SICILIAN COMEDIES

SICILIAN COMEDIES

Cap and Bells
and
Man, Beast and Virtue

TWO PLAYS BY
LUIGI PIRANDELLO

Performing Arts Journal Publications
New York City

SICILIAN COMEDIES
© 1983 Copyright by Performing Arts Journal Publications
© 1983 Copyright by Giorgio Moscon, Executor, Pirandello Estate, Via Luigi Settembrini 9, Rome, Italy
© Translation of *Cap and Bells* copyright by Norman A. Bailey
© Translation of *Man, Beast and Virtue* copyright by Roger W. Oliver

First Edition
All rights reserved
No part of this publication may be reproduced or transmitted in any form or by any means, electronic or mechanical, including photocopy, recording, or any information storage or retrieval system now known or to be invented, without permission in writing from the publishers, except by a reviewer who wishes to quote brief passages in connection with a review written for inclusion in a magazine, newspaper, or broadcast.

Library of Congress Cataloging in Publication Data
Sicilian Comedies
Library of Congress Catalog Card No.: 82-62097
ISBN: 0-933826-50-8 (cloth)
ISBN: 0-933826-51-6 (paper)

All rights reserved under the International and Pan-American Copyright Conventions. For information, write to Performing Arts Journal Publications, 325 Spring Street, Room 318, New York, N.Y. 10013.

Professionals and amateurs are warned that the plays appearing herein are fully protected under the Copyright Laws of the United States and all other countries of the Copyright Union. All rights including professional, amateur, motion picture, recitation, lecturing, public readings, radio and television broadcasting, and the rights of translation into foreign languages, are strictly reserved. All inquiries concerning performance rights to *Cap and Bells* and *Man, Beast and Virtue* should be addressed to Toby Cole, Agent; 468 Riverside Drive, New York, N.Y. 10027.

Design: Gautam Dasgupta
Printed in the United States of America

Publication of this book has been made possible in part by a grant from the National Endowment for the Arts, Washington, D.C., a federal agency, and public funds received from the New York State Council on the Arts.

PAJ Playscripts/General Editors:
Bonnie Marranca and Gautam Dasgupta

The translator of *Man, Beast and Virtue* would like to thank John Olon for his assistance in the preparation of an earlier version of the translation.—R. O.

CONTENTS

Introduction by Olga Ragusa   7

    CAP AND BELLS   17

    MAN, BEAST AND VIRTUE   51

INTRODUCTION

Olga Ragusa

Cap and Bells and *Man, Beast and Virtue* are pre-*Six Characters* Pirandello. This means that in neither is the theatre as the place where plays are performed at issue. They are, as it were, unframed: what happens in them does not happen in a theatre but in a real-life locale which the setting on stage simulates. Their characters are not "created realities," Characters with a capital "C," but persons, individuals such as exist in the external, material world and are impersonated by actors whose self-awareness, if they have any beyond their professional expertise, never rises to self-expression. The audience, when the play begins, has before it the traditional enclosed space from which the fourth wall has been removed. The author has no role in these plays except that of the omnipotent, invisible fashioner into a coherent, stageable whole of fictional material that imitates life.

Cap and Bells is set in an unnamed city in the interior of Sicily, a social environment described with venom by Signora Ignazia, who in *Tonight We Improvise* is forced to live in it, as inhabited by men and women "burning with an instinctive rage that makes them savage to one another," "frightening wolves" more than human beings. It is perhaps the principal aspect of Sicily that Pirandello's work has contributed to making familiar: the Sicily of "taciturn apathy, suspicious mistrust, and jealousy," as he had written apropos his native Agrigento in *The Old and the Young*, the Sicily whose heritage meant a rigidly formal and immobile social structure, with its accompanying sense of reticence and secretiveness, its private language full of allusions, and the blocking of the individual psyche with the perennial danger of a sudden and irremediable explosion. Without bearing this ethnic background in mind, both in the historical world of the late nineteenth century and in Pirandello's fictional world, we run the risk of misunderstanding this play.

Il berretto a sonagli (*'A birritta cu' i ciancianeddi*), with the title in parenthesis as Pirandello wanted it for fear that the Sicilian words would prove a stumbling block—this is how *Cap and Bells* was first announced to the public on the earliest handbills. It was written in less than a week in the summer of 1916, a play that was "born" and not "made," as Pirandello himself put it to underline its spontaneity. It had its premiere in Rome on July 27, 1917. Together with three other plays, Pirandello contributed it to his friend, the playwright Martoglio's project to create an "art theatre" in Sicilian dialect, which would counteract the raucous, primitive, low comedy being imported into continental Italy by acting companies more intent on the immediate success of boisterous laughter than on representing the varied and authentic life of the island. One of the Sicilian actors, however, escaped Pirandello's condemnation: Angelo Musco, whom E. Gordon Craig would call "the greatest actor in the world" and of whom André Antoine would say that he had never seen such an overflowing of sheer comic energy on any stage. It was for Musco that Pirandello wrote *Think It Over, Giacomino!*, *Liolà*, and *The Jar*, in addition to *Cap and Bells*. Although published in Pirandello's Italian version as early as 1918 and included in the first collection of *Maschere Nude* in 1920, *Cap and Bells* was not performed in Italian until 1928 when it was staged by Pirandello's own Company with its star Marta Abba and Lamberto Picasso (one of Pirandello's greatest interpreters) in the two leading roles.

In a letter to Martoglio, recently published, Pirandello prides himself on having created three characters for Musco that would have made any actor's fortune: Agostino Toti (in *Think It Over, Giacomino!*), Liolà, and Nociu Pampina, i.e., Ciampa, as he will be renamed in Italian. Indeed, these three are the first major male characters in Pirandello's theatre on its way to the discovery of the character without an author. The mild-mannered but intransigent Professor Toti, the exuberant Liolà, the hard pressed Ciampa, attest to Musco's versatility as an actor and to his liberating effect on Pirandello's talent. All three are dialecticians, village philosophers, critics of things as they are, disrupters of accepted morality, creators of a new one. Their roles were exactly suited to Musco who, in the strict distribution of parts which typifies acting companies such as his, was cast as the *brillante* (Pirandello's "raisonneur") and not as the *primo attore* (male lead, with the connotation of tragic or romantic hero).

Like the protagonists of the two short stories that are the narrative precedents of *Cap and Bells* ("Certi obblighi" [Certain Obligations] and "La verità" [The Truth]), Ciampa is a wronged husband who is capable of tolerating his wife's infidelity as long as he is not forced to reveal that he knows that others believe he is aware of it. Once this thin line is crossed, however, it becomes his obligation, his duty, to redeem his honor by killing his wife (and her lover if caught *in flagrante*). This is the iron code that operates at all levels of society, establishing a bond of empathy and solidarity between the men in the community and recognized as compelling and inescapable by the women as well.

The first scenes of the play focus on the women's world, on the claustrophobic interior of an over-furnished provincial parlor that is emblematic of Signora Beatrice's state of mind. The wife of Ciampa's employer, she is convinced that her husband is the lover of Ciampa's wife. Were the play not so unmistakably Ciampa's, a case might be made at this point for reading it as Signora Beatrice's story.

Pirandello's own judgment of Beatrice is implicit in the outcome of the play, and is stated in so many words at the beginning in the stage directions that describe her. Like others of Pirandello's sterile women protagonists, she is fragile, self-centered, irresponsible, possibly through no fault of her own, but in any case sufficiently so to become disruptive and socially dangerous. Egged on by the junk-dealer La Saracena, she is determined to set a trap for her husband and thus to "free" herself, to cast off bonds that like a tight garment (in one of Pirandello's stories it is a frockcoat) prevent her from breathing. La Saracena is a witch-like figure, the classic dispenser of love potions and mysterious brews, the spreader of rumors and the go-between in shady deals, an ever-present component of a primitive community. She is pitted against Fana, Beatrice's old family-servant, who counsels caution and resignation: what Beatrice sees as her freedom, Fana warns, will actually be her ruin.

The interchanges between this trio of women give the first scene of the play a surprising ring of topicality, almost as though it had been written as a mini-demonstration of a consciousness-raising session for women. La Saracena's indignant derision of Fana's position is necessarily read today as more than an accurate bit of local color. It is instantly felt to have the status of rallying-cry for the redress of wrongs long endured. But the issue of the play is not the achievement of Beatrice's "liberation." In the microcosm that *Cap and Bells* sets on stage, no one has unqualified freedom, everyone has obligations to be met. It is this fact, the existence of this basic contract, that Ciampa comes to recall to the mind of those who have forgotten it, principal among them Beatrice. Her transgression will have to be punished, but because, as it turns out, its intended effect is blocked in time, her punishment will be ambiguous, returning her—after a cooling-off interval—to the position she held before.

Ciampa has two entrances in the play. When he first steps on stage in the course of Act I, he already bears the marks of Pirandello's typically "different," disturbed protagonist. When he reappears in Act II, after La Saracena's plan has been implemented, the ravages of suffering have increased: he has been virtually destroyed, the mask torn from his face, his existential suffering exposed. His power to reason, however, remains unimpaired. In Act I he expounds his theory of the "three springs" that regulate men's actions in their relations with one another; in Act II he applies the theory to his own plight with great astuteness. After trying reasoning and persuasion in vain, he turns the "crazy key" like mad, so hard that Beatrice is hypnotized into acting insane. Thus her accusations will appear to be the ravings of an unbalanced mind, and the ritual blood-bath will be averted.

Yet in spite of the conclusion, which in the spirit of comedy celebrates accommodation, the ending of *Cap and Bells* is far from happy. Ciampa's bitterness, like "Henry IV's," is corrosive. How he would love to get out into the streets and play the madman! How he would love to spit out the truth in people's faces! He despises them all, remaining frightfully alone, a man who has understood the game and gets no comfort from it. The curtain falls on his burst of ferocious, savage, desperate laughter.

Pirandello's 1917 letters to Martoglio throw light on some of the difficulties inherent in the play and already encountered in the earliest rehearsals and performances. There were first of all complaints from the first actor cast as Ciampa (not Musco) about the unamanageable length and complication of his lines, and at the same time about his having to "stand by" while the other characters were reciting their lines. There was Pirandello's fear that the audience, accustomed to going to see the Sicilian companies and Musco especially to have a good laugh, would not be able to take the play seriously. And there was his apprehension that Musco in particular would overact, abusing such gestures as the turning of the three springs, or, at the opposite extreme, that for some reason he would fail to come up with the requisite sustained devilish verve and thus cause the whole thing to fall flat. For *Cap and Bells* undoubtedly requires both an extraordinary actor in the main role and impeccable ensemble work. For this reason the best performances have been by general agreement those beginning in 1936, in the Neapolitan translation of Eduardo De Filippo, the playwright and actor, with Eduardo himself playing Ciampa, his sister Titina Beatrice, and his brother Peppino the head of police.

Walter Littlefield, who reviewed the American premiere of the play for the *New York Times* in November 1931 (this was not in English translation but in the original Italian), tried hard to be informative and fair, but would have preferred the play to be "more Sicilian, much more tragic" and found that "the last curtain left things rather in narrative, if not in artistic, complexity." Desmond Pratt, who in the *Yorkshire Post* reviewed its first performance in English, in Frederick May's translation and production at the Leeds (England) Civic Theatre in January 1958, was more perceptive and polemical (possibly because there was no language barrier for him). He was enthusiastic about May's staging with its almost entire absence of sets, and had the highest words of praise for Philip Stone's Ciampa, who in the second act reached "a theatrical climax so powerful as to have completely hushed last night's audience."

In the United States *Cap and Bells* was apparently first produced in English in July 1981 (although there is a microfilm of a translation by Winifred Smith in the Columbia University Libraries dated 1957, and an English version by John and Marion Field published in 1974). It was staged, in Norman A. Bailey's translation, by the Rutgers Theatre Company as part of its summer season, and hailed in various local New Jersey papers as an early Pirandello which presents the playwright as already at the height of his creative force. The *New York Times* reviewer spoke of "Latinate brio and a bitter laugh," of "a grotesque web of comic double-takes." Other reviewers, interestingly enough, were struck especially by the figure of Beatrice and the female world around her.

Man, Beast and Virtue is a very different kind of play from *Cap and Bells*. Pirandello called it an "apologue," while he had been content with the generic designation "comedy"—the Italian catch-all equivalent to the English "play"—for *Cap and Bells*. An apologue is a moral fable, a tale mostly about animals or inanimate objects, that, by acting like human beings, reflect the follies of mankind; it is to be read allegorically, not mimetically. Inasmuch as the apologue, like the parable (which is the term Pirandello used for *It Is So*), is thought of as a medium for teaching some truth, *Man, Beast and Virtue,* which is more than anything else a farce and an off-color one at that, has given rise to considerable perplexity. Its first performance on May 6, 1919, was such a flop that Antonio Gandusio, the well-known comic actor whose company produced it, erased it from his memory to the point of not even mentioning it in his later book of reminiscences about his life in the theatre. One of the reviewers the next day called it "disgusting" and wondered how Pirandello could have reverted to such traditional nonsense after having revolutionized the Italian theatre and the figure of the husband on stage in particular. (*Man, Beast and Virtue*, it must be remembered, followed not only *Cap and Bells* and *It Is So*, but such other idea plays as *The Pleasure of Honesty* and *The Rules of the Game* as well.) Its subsequent production history was to disprove its disastrous beginning, but difficulties in placing and judging it would persist.

The play is set in a seaport town, "it doesn't matter which," Pirandello adds, leaving its geographical location unspecified as befits the abstract aspects of its genre. But it might well be the Porto Empedocle of his father's sulphur business and of his own early fiction. The characters that crowd into the modest parlor and study of the private teacher, Signor Paolino, are the familiar ones of Pirandello's regional settings. They form a gallery of grotesques: the pharmacist, who lives in an adjoining apartment with his brother the doctor and comes daily to wheedle his morning coffee from Paolino's housekeeper; she, the usual wary and suspicious guardian of her master's physical well-being; the first of Paolino's pupils to arrive, two stolid monsters, one a "black billy goat," the other "a big ape with glasses." Animal imagery abounds in the stage directions here and later in the play, a further sign that we are close to the small-town provincial world of Pirandello's brand of Sicilian realism.

Like other "raisonneurs" in Pirandello's repertoire, Paolino, too, is a philosopher of sorts, as suits his profession and his impetuous and irritable, volatile and explosive nature. It is surprising that his lines in Act I on the word "hypocrite" (actor, comedian, in Greek) should not have joined the small group of Pirandello's frequently quoted statements on the concepts of being and seeming, reality and illusion: read immediately after Ciampa's lines on the "three springs" in Acts I and II of *Cap and Bells* they reveal their unmistakable derivation from the same matrix. But there is little time for Paolino to develop and display his pedagogical abilities or his sophistical subtlety. He finds himself in a situation that requires an immediate practical solution, a situation that is neither specifically Sicilian nor specifically Pirandellian but has its roots squarely in folk humor as filtered through the long and subversive tradition of the bawdy tale, the fabliau or the Boccaccio-esque novella.

Paolino makes much of Signora Perella's plight as the neglected wife of a sea captain, and of his having chivalrously rallied to the defense of her "virtue." Obviously had it not be he, such is the implication, it would have been someone else, someone less appreciative of her "virtue." For he is no Don Giovanni, no hard-hearted exploiter of women, no arrogant village philanderer (like Turiddu in *Cavalleria rusticana*). He is genuinely solicitous of her, shares in her anguish, never has a hard word for her. True, he is "transparent" (as he was originally described in the cast of characters), he and no one else may be deceived by his self-justifications, but this does not seem to impair the relationship with Signora Perella. His concern now is only to find a remedy for an unwanted pregnancy, not the extreme remedy of abortion (for this play is no tragedy, nor is Pirandello interested in social criticism), but the more ambiguous remedy of making sure that the child will pass as that of its mother's wedded husband. The situation defies the laws of sexual jealousy: the lover must play pander to his mistress.

Characters in comedy are generally stereotypes, reassuring because they present few problems in being judged. This is not entirely so in *Man, Beast and Virtue*, in which the basic triangle situation is familiar but the individuals caught in it less so. Besides being the cuckolded husband, Captain Perella is the "beast": his voracious appetite, his adulterous affair in Naples, his tyrannical treatment of his wife and son, as well as verbal references in the text, make this abundantly explicit. But how is Paolino "man," that is, man in general, and what "virtue" does Signora Perella represent? In the narrative precedent of the play, "Richiamo all'obbligo" (A Call Back to Duty, the duty being the marital obligation), the wife never appears in person but is only evoked in Paolino's inner monologue or in his excited dialogue with the doctor. In the play instead, at her first entrance, in an instance of those frequent stage directions in Pirandello that go beyond the usual bare instructions and touch upon aspects of characterization that it is a challenge to translate into the visual language of the stage, Signora Perella is described in great detail. She is virtue, modesty, chasteness incarnate; but not beauteous virtue. She is dowdy and stick-like, as though it were not she speaking, writes Pirandello, but the invisible puppeteer that makes her move. She lacks charm and like Paolino, in spite of his restless ratiocination, psychological depth. Neither has undergone one of those shattering experiences—madness, amnesia, betrayal, *anagnorisis*—that distinguish Pirandello's most powerful dramatic situations. Paolino has seduced Signora Perella, but there is no hint whatsoever of what her feelings might have been; her infidelity is a "given," an inescapable and to all appearances joyless fact of nature, accompanied by no feeling of guilt or of liberation but only fear of punishment now that it can no longer be kept secret.

Atypically for Pirandello's female characters, she has no maternal feelings, whether for her son Nonò, the third child-monster of the play, or for the baby to be born. In Act II when Paolino decks her out, arranging her dress, supervising her hair-do, applying her makeup, so as to make her enticing for the "beast," she succeeds only in becoming more ridiculous, actually laughable, as Captain Perella himself demonstrates. The double vision of *umorismo*—the perception of the incongruous followed by its feeling or sentiment, what things look like as opposed to what they must feel like—does not operate where there is no possibility of identification. As other works do in which the peasant world persists in its repellent and grotesque aspects, with its degraded view of human actions and motives (in *The Festival of Our Lord of the Ship,* for instance), so *Man, Beast and Virtue* points to what we might call the Pirandellian version of Expressionism.

Productions of *Man, Beast and Virtue* have, not unexpectedly, emphasized its farcical aspects. It appears to have been first performed in English in December 1926, in a translation by Alice Rohe, *Say It with Flowers* (the reference being to the flower pots with which the next morning Signora Perella announces her successful "seduction" of her husband). This production was part of the "milkman's matinees," midnight performances for "the tired business man too tired to go home," staged by Brock Pemberton, who had in 1922 introduced Pirandello to America with *Six Characters* and had the following year mounted a Pirandello Season. Brooks Atkinson, reviewing it in the *New York Times,* called it "the type of skit much relished by staid Americans taking a moral holiday in Paris." For the *New York Telegraph* reviewer it was "a highly amusing combination of banter and burlesque . . . a frisky and risqué story . . . The moral, if any, is that you *can* eat your cake and have it too." It is because of the cake (which contains the aphrodisiac that makes the Captain perform his duty) that the play ran afoul of the censor in England. Performed by the New College Dramatic Society in Oxford, May 1957, in Frederick May's translation, it had to be cut on the spot (as the *Oxford Times* reports) on order to the "small man who had been sitting through the play with a script and a torch" and finally identified himself as the representative of the Lord Chamberlain.

An unusual performance was the one given in February 1934 at the Yiddish Art Theatre in New York with Joseph Buloff as Paolino and Paul Baratov as the Captain. In its Yiddish dress the play was known as *He, She and the Ox.* With still another title, *Call It Virtue,* it was performed at the Astor Place Playhouse in New York, in March 1963. The translation was the one by Edward Eager, which had also been used at the Stratford Theatre Royal in London, in February 1958. Howard Taubman, reviewing it for the *New York Times,* was far from enthusiastic. He found the play tiresome and frivolous ("its substance would have trouble covering the head of a pin") and the production so overemphatic that "the jest, such as it is, turns ponderous." Even his last sentence held out little hope: "It is possible, though not probable, that a more sophisticated and subtle production might have discovered a little more laughter in the thin piece." The challenge was taken up in 1981 when Alfred

Drake reworked Edward Eager's translation, revising, rewriting, and adapting it for an Off-Broadway Workshop Production at The Players in New York.

There was also a film version, with the dead-pan comic actor Totò as Paolino, the French actress Viviane Romance as Signora Perella, and Orson Welles as the Captain. Produced in Italy in 1953, it changed the ending of the play, omitting the aphrodisiac, having the Captain return to his wife in a rediscovery of her attractiveness, and sending Paolino off to find consolation in the arms of the town prostitute.

Finally, two decades earlier, in 1931, there has been a most unusual production of *Man, Beast and Virtue* in Paris, so unusual, in fact, that it warrants being taken out of chronological sequence here to receive a privileged place in the history of Pirandello's progressive conquest of acting space. The performance was in French, with Marta Abba as Signora Perella and two popular French actors (of *Topaze* fame) in the leading male roles. Around this production Pirandello staged one of those publicity stunts that had just shortly before made the other two plays of the trilogy of the theatre-within-the theatre, *Each in His Own Way* and *Tonight We Improvise*, spill over into the theatre lobby, the orchestra, off-stage, and even into the street in front of the theatre building itself.

An interview in *Le Figaro* on the day of the opening and an insert into the program handed out to the audience announced Pirandello's rebellion against being typecast as the inventor of Pirandellism and his determination to renounce his name if this would help him to regain the freedom of his imagination as a writer. It is one of Pirandello's many declarations of the primacy of the imagination in his art ("My works are born of living images, the inexhaustible and perennial source of art"). And it is a sign of the high esteem in which he held this play, and of his sense of the coherence of his whole *oeuvre*, that he should have chosen to repeat his self-declaration on this occasion.

CAP AND BELLS

A Play in Two Acts

Translated by Norman A. Bailey

CHARACTERS

Ciampa, a clerk
Beatrice Fiorica
Assunta La Bella, her mother
Fifi La Bella, her brother
Spano, Commissioner of Police
La Saracena, old clothes dealer
Fana, old servant of Beatrice
Nina Ciampa, young wife of Ciampa

Today. A small town in the interior of Sicily.

ACT I

Salon in the Fiorica house. Furnished in a rich but provincial style. There is a large door up center and two other doors stage right and stage left, with hangings. When the curtain rises Beatrice is seated on a divan, weeping. La Saracena, seated across from her, stares at her annoyed. Fana is standing by the upstage door.

FANA: (*Pointing to Beatrice. To La Saracena.*) You see what you've done? Are you happy now? Ruining such a lovely family! Aren't you ashamed?
LA SARACENA: (*A large, terrifying woman in her forties, wearing full silk skirts and a silkscarf with long fringes. Rising.*) What the devil do you think you're saying? Ashamed? Me? And what of the shame that has fallen on your poor mistress?
BEATRICE: (*A woman about thirty, pale, hysterical, given to sudden furies. Continuing to weep. To Fana.*) Anyway, must I account for my actions to you?
FANA: To me? No, Signora. I am merely here to serve you. But we must all account to God.
BEATRICE: (*Furious.*) Get out! Go to the kitchen! Go on about your business!
LA SARACENA: (*Grasping Fana by the arm.*) No, no, wait, my fine lady. We all have souls, masters and servants alike. And what about *your* conscience? What sort of conscience do you have, that you can see your mistress weep tears of blood, suffer the tortures of the damned and say: "Patience, it is nothing, God wills it." Is that conscience?
FANA: Yes, it is for those who fear God.

BEATRICE: I suppose I should let myself be deceived, pray for my husband and say thank you?
FANA: It doesn't do any good to fight with those who are stronger than we. Be patient, Signora, be patient. A pleasant face and a cheerful manner is what brings our husbands home.
LA SARACENA: Oh, wonderful! And if all women acted like that I shudder to think of the advantage that men would take of us!
FANA: He treats her like a queen! Her husband is prudent and respects her, and she lacks for nothing.
BEATRICE: Will you be quiet? Prudence, eh? Respect, abundance, a full house. And what does he do outside the house? And what about my peace? And my heart? Must I keep everything inside me, and hide what goes on outside?
LA SARACENA: (*To Fana.*) You call that conscience? Where I come from we call it hypocrisy. And anyway, did you or did you not come to get me?
FANA: I was ordered to. I had nothing to do with it.
LA SARACENA: Wonderful! And wasn't I ordered also? I get the message: "Saracena, help me! My husband, etc., etc., so on and so on. Tell me if it is true. My house is hell. I must leave at all costs!" Did you send this?
BEATRICE: Yes, yes, I must break it off, at once, once and for all!
FANA: Oh, dear Mother of God!
LA SARACENA: What do you mean, Mother of God? In a house where jealousy has entered? It's destroyed, finished! A perpetual earthquake! Just think if there were children also!
FANA: That's just the trouble. There aren't any children.
LA SARACENA: And so? Why should she split her body, this poor woman? She says she must leave.
FANA: Yes, but she weeps as she says it.
BEATRICE: I'm weeping from fury! If I had him here I'd chop him into pieces! Tell me, Saracena, is it true that I can trap them tomorrow?
LA SARACENA: Like two turtledoves in their nest. At what time does he return?
BEATRICE: At ten!
LA SARACENA: Then I tell you that at ten-thirty, Signora, you will have them both, wriggling and squirming! Give the commissioner your denunciation. I'll take care of the rest . . . But first tell me something. Is it true that your husband is passing through Palermo before going to Catania?
BEATRICE: Yes, why?
LA SARACENA: Well, because . . . Because . . . No, never mind.
BEATRICE: Tell me, tell me. What do you know?
LA SARACENA: Well, I know of a certain little gift that he promised to bring her from Palermo.
BEATRICE: To her? A gift?
LA SARACENA: A beautiful necklace, with pendants.

FANA: You're not a woman, you're a devil!

LA SARACENA: Write it, write the denunciation!

BEATRICE: No . . . no . . . it's better . . . Oh God, I'm going to explode. It's better to have the commissioner come here. Commissioner Spano is a friend; you know, he owes everything to my father—may he rest in peace. He'll tell me what to do. Go on, Saracena, run, bring him here.

FANA: Signora, for the love of God! Signora, think of the scandal.

BEATRICE: I don't care about anything!

FANA: At least wait until the master returns.

BEATRICE: I'm leaving him! I'm leaving him! I'm leaving him! Go on, Saracena, don't lose any more time.

FANA: (*Holding La Saracena back.*) Wait a moment. Wait, Signora, of him . . . Pardon me—the husband of that good lady—if she is—of him, of Ciampa, have you thought of him?

BEATRICE: Everything, everything, I've thought of everything, even of him; don't interfere! I know where to send him!

LA SARACENA: What's the need? Why send him away? He's used to it. Take my word, the moment the master returns and goes to the bank, he'll pick up his hat and leave.

FANA: Who? Ciampa? You're crazy. She wants to make you believe, Signora, that Ciampa suspects everything but keeps still.

LA SARACENA: Keep quiet yourself. What do you know?

FANA: You're wrong, you couldn't be more wrong.

LA SARACENA: Don't be a fool, eh? Open your eyes. Pim! Pam! What do you mean? To see the woman with bracelets up to her ears, four rings on each finger; tomorrow he'll see her wearing the necklace with pendants, and what then? Eh? She bought them with her pin money? Wake up! When the master's in the bank, where's Ciampa? Always in the middle of the street, with his nose in the air, wandering around here and there with nothing to do.

FANA: He's ordered to go out! He's ordered! What do you want him to do, the poor man? Anyhow, everyone knows that when Ciampa leaves the bank he barricades the door to his apartment with an iron bar.

LA SARACENA: The president lifts it.

FANA: He locks it with a chain!

LA SARACENA: And so? The president has a key.

BEATRICE: Oh, oh, are you finally going to finish. Fana, get out of here and don't interfere. (*To La Saracena.*) I'll have Ciampa brought here and send him on a trip tonight. No . . . you, Fana, come here. Now . . . do you understand? Can I trust you?

FANA: Signora mia, you stab me to the heart! I carried you in my arms when you were a child! And now you don't want to trust me? (*Starts to cry.*)

BEATRICE: Now, now; now, now; don't cry, for heaven's sake!

FANA: Signora, you have a brother; you have a mother, Signora. Go to them, ask them for advice—they are your own blood, they wouldn't betray you!
BEATRICE: That's enough! I don't want to see anyone! Go and bring Ciampa here, quickly! And you, Saracena, Commissioner Spano. Ask him in my name to come here; right now, at once.
LA SARACENA: On the contrary, madam.
BEATRICE: What do you mean? On the contrary?
LA SARACENA: (*Pointing to Fana.*) Send her for the commissioner. I'll take care of Ciampa.
BEATRICE: (*To Fana.*) Do you know where to find the commissioner?
FANA: If you command me, I'll find him.
LA SARACENA: Whatever happens, Signora, don't worry. You never know what's going to come out of a situation like this. You wouldn't even dream it! I'm going to give you, Signora, one little lesson, and that's all. Four years ago I kicked my husband out of the door. He came crawling back eventually and now he doesn't dare go out except when I fix him with the evil eye, like this. How he trembles! A little lesson, nothing more. Kick him a good one in the pants! It's a pleasure, anyway. But I'm going. You're certain now, eh? You're absolutely certain? I don't want to . . .
BEATRICE: Absolutely! Completely!
LA SARACENA: Tomorrow?
BEATRICE: Tomorrow.
LA SARACENA: All right. I'm off to get Ciampa. (*She starts out by the up center door but before she gets there the doorbell rings loudly.*) Someone's at the door!
BEATRICE: (*To Fana, who is going to open the door.*) Wait. It may be my brother. If it is, not a word about all this. (*Makes her a sign to be quiet.*)
FANA: If the Signora doesn't want me to talk I won't talk. (*She leaves by the up center door.*)
BEATRICE: I've asked him to come to arrange for Ciampa to leave.
LA SARACENA: I tell you it's not necessary. The fewer people who know about this, Signora, the better. Even Fana . . .
BEATRICE: Fana is loyal, don't worry. As far as my brother is concerned, leave him to me. I've got an idea.

(*Fifi La Bella enters from the center door. He is about 24 years old, a handsome, elegant youth.*)

LA SARACENA: (*Bowing.*) Your servant, Signor.
FIFI: (*Looking at her with dislike.*) You here?
LA SARACENA: I was just about to leave.
BEATRICE: Yes, yes, go quickly. I'll be waiting for Ciampa.
LA SARACENA: He'll be here. Your servant. (*She leaves by the center door.*)
FIFI: What are you doing with that witch?

BEATRICE: I? Nothing. She came to do me a service.
FIFI: Don't you know that a good woman can't receive her without compromising herself?
BEATRICE: Oh, of course! Because she knows all the shameful and detestable deeds you men commit, you're all afraid she'll tell your wives and your mothers.
FIFI: Bravo. Very good. Go on like that and I flatter myself I know where *you'll* end up.
BEATRICE: Don't worry about me, I know where I'll end up. If you men had your way we'd be kept in the dark about everything!
FIFI: You're full of poison today!
BEATRICE: Did you bring the money?
FIFI: I brought it.
BEATRICE: I remember when you used quite a different tone. I remember when you needed the money. (*Imitating his humble and sugary voice.*) "Dear little sister, for the love of God, help me. You who are so good, save me! I was gambling, I lost it all: save me from dishonor!" And I had to go running to that "witch," to that woman whom I cannot receive without compromising myself—for you, for you I did it—to send her to Palermo to pawn a pair of earrings and a bracelet.
FIFI: Ah, you want the money to get them out of hock?
BEATRICE: Come on, come on, where is it?
FIFI: (*Getting out his wallet.*) There's a little bit lacking.
BEATRICE: I knew it! How much?
FIFI: If you could have waited a little bit longer, not much, maybe another two weeks . . . I don't understand why this sudden hurry.
BEATRICE: I want to have the earrings and the bracelet again by tomorrow. I've sent for Ciampa so he can go for them immediately.
FIFI: Does your husband suspect they are missing? Doesn't he return tomorrow?
BEATRICE: Exactly! How clever! That's why I have to have them.
FIFI: Um, perhaps now I understand. You want to appear with all your jewels tomorrow to receive your husband.
BEATRICE: But of course! I must make him welcome! Oh my, what a festive occasion! (*The doorbell sounds.*) There's Ciampa. Give it here, give me the money. How much is missing?
FIFI: (*Taking the money out of his wallet.*) Who knows? Count it yourself. I think there are three bills of a hundred . . .
BEATRICE: . . . and one of fifty. You still owe me a hundred and fifty lire!
FIFI: I told you, if you could have waited . . .
BEATRICE: It's all right, it's all right, I'll get the rest. You can go now.
FANA: (*From the center door.*) Ciampa's here. Can he come in?
BEATRICE: Yes, tell him to . . . No, wait, come here a moment. (*She draws*

Fana apart and whispers to her.) Go immediately where I told you.

FANA: (*Very softly.*) To the commissioner?

BEATRICE: Tell him to come here immediately. If he comes too soon have him wait in the study. Take the key and go at once.

FANA: I'm going, Signora, I'm going . . . (*She leaves.*)

FIFI: Is it possible to know what the devil you're up to? What is all this mystery?

BEATRICE: Quiet, Ciampa's here.

(*Ciampa enters from the up center door. A man about 45 years old, he wears a long, threadbare coat. He has long mustaches and acute, mobile, slightly insane eyes. He keeps a pen behind his right ear.*)

CIAMPA: I kiss your hands, Signora. My dear Signor Fifi . . . Ready for your commands, Signora.

FIFI: Always "ready," aren't you, my dear Ciampa?

CIAMPA: Yes, Signor. Always turning here and there, like Christ on the cross. Always ready. What else would I be here but a humble servant?

BEATRICE: Oh come now! You, a servant? We're all masters here, dear Ciampa, without distinction; you, Fifi, my mother, *I* . . . *your wife*, what do I know? My husband, Fana: all equal! And I'm not sure that I'm not lower than all of you!

CIAMPA: Signora! For God's sake! What are you saying?

FIFI: Let her talk! She says that, because all women, according to her . . .

BEATRICE: Ah no, not all, not all: *certain* women! Because others, my dear brother, know how to take things into their hands and revenge themselves, even in the streets, if necessary!

CIAMPA: If you'll excuse me, Signora? You also named my wife?

BEATRICE: No, I spoke in general: Fana, my mother, *I* . . . *your wife* . . .

FIFI: All women, and all equal!

CIAMPA: Pardon me. I ask your pardon also, Signor Fifi. But it seems to me that my wife, even in a discourse of this kind—general . . . Like Pilate in the *Credo* . . . I am at your service, and everything is fine, of course; but my wife is in excellent hands, happy and at home, and it isn't necessary for anyone to speak of her, either in praise or otherwise.

BEATRICE: Good Lord, you really are jealous! You can't even hear her named without going off in a huff.

CIAMPA: No, Signora. It's merely a question of principle. Women, sardines and anchovies. The latter under tin and oil, the former under lock and key. Here it is! (*He takes out a key and shows them.*)

FIFI: (*Laughing.*) A fine principle for my sister!

CIAMPA: (*Putting his hands on his chest.*) To each his own, Signor Fifi.

BEATRICE: (*To Fifi.*) It's possible that, while you watch the door, the window

may be open!
CIAMPA: Oh yes, Signora. But the duty of the husband is to lock the door.
BEATRICE: I never realized you were such a terrible person!
CIAMPA: Terrible? Me? Why no! Why? I like everything to be cleared up in advance. Now for the window—the door is locked. Look outside! Take the air! There's just one little thing. I don't want the neighbors to come to me saying, "Ciampa, your wife is about to break her neck trying to jump out of the window!" It seems to me there is nothing terrible in all this. The man knows that the woman has to take a little air at the window. The woman knows that the man has to lock the door. That's all. What does the Signora wish of me?
BEATRICE: Oh, Fifi . . . you understand, I have to talk to Ciampa.
FIFI: So? Why do you want me to leave?
BEATRICE: Can I talk in front of you?
FIFI: And why not? Talk, talk away. I've repaid what I owed you.
BEATRICE: All right, all right. Now. Sit down, Ciampa. I need your help. A faithful man like you. One of the family . . . *and more.*
CIAMPA: Through my devotion . . .
BEATRICE: . . . through your devotion, and *everything else.*
CIAMPA: Signora, I must warn you, I'm not a slow person.
BEATRICE: What do you mean?
CIAMPA: Nothing. It seems as if you speak today . . . I don't know . . . as if you've been eating lemons this morning.
BEATRICE: Lemons? Honey! I've been eating honey this morning! Anyway, what do you mean by saying . . .
CIAMPA: Oh, good God, I'm not speaking of words, Signora. Let's not be childish! You're trying to make me search beneath the words to find something that the words do not say.
BEATRICE: But where? When? You got out of the wrong side of the bed this morning.
CIAMPA: I appeal to you, Signor Fifi. What does she mean by saying that I am *more* than a member of the family? I answer: "Through my devotion." And she comes back: "Through your devotion, and *everything else.*" What does this *everything else* mean? What does she mean by saying that we are all masters here, without distinction, *including my wife*? I am the one who got out of the bed on the wrong side? Why do you say these things against me?
FIFI: Not against you! Against everyone! This is a serious matter!
BEATRICE: Would someone like to tell me what I said? Am I not allowed to speak any more?
CIAMPA: It's not that, dear lady. Would you like me to explain everything? The instrument is ready.
BEATRICE: The instrument? What instrument?
CIAMPA: The social spring, Signora. You must know that we all have three

springs, in our heads, like in a watch. (*With his right hand he motions as if he were winding a watch, first on the right side of his forehead, then in the middle, then on the left side.*) The serious, the social, and the insane. Above all, since we must live in society, we use the social spring. That's why it's in the middle. Otherwise we would eat each other raw. I would devour . . . as an example . . . Signor Fifi. And what do I do instead? I bow, I approach him with my hand extended, I say: "Oh, how happy I am to see you, my dear Signor Fifi." Do you understand, Signora? But the moment may arrive when the waters get a little muddied. And now . . . now, I approach, turning the serious key, and I speak seriously, honestly, saying what I really think and what I really know, without circumlocution, without hypocrisy. And then if things do not work out, Signora, then I turn the insane spring, the light goes out from my eyes, and I no longer know what I am doing.

FIFI: Marvelous! Marvelous! Bravo, Ciampa!

CIAMPA: You Signora, at this time, you'll excuse me, you should have been turning furiously—for this business of yours!! (I don't want to know what it is)—either the serious spring or the insane one, because you have inside you the buzzing of a hundred hornets! Nevertheless you insist on speaking to me with the social spring. What happens? What happens is that the words I find in your mouth come from the social spring, but they sound false. Do I explain myself? You hide them from me, I will search for them. Tell Signor Fifi to go at once . . . I beg you myself, Signor Fifi . . . leave us.

BEATRICE: Why no, why? Let him stay.

FIFI: Will you do me the favor of letting me stay and listen?

CIAMPA: (*With intensity.*) Because you, Signora—will you permit me?—on the right side of your forehead, you should give a twist to the serious spring and speak with me *seriously*: for your good and for mine!

BEATRICE: Of course! That's what I intend to do!

CIAMPA: Ah, then it's all right. Everything's fine. But take care, Signora, take care, when the serious spring is not wound up in time sometimes the insane spring will wind by itself. Be warned!

FIFI: It seems to me, my dear Ciampa, that you're the one who's beginning to sound out of tune.

BEATRICE: Frankly, I don't understand any of this . . .

CIAMPA: I ask your pardon. (*With a feeling of sudden improvisation.*) Signor Fifi, my father's forehead was once split wide open.

FIFI: What does your father have to do with all this?

CIAMPA: It happened when he was a child—an accident—my father, instead of saving his head, saved his hands, do you see? When he found himself falling, he immediately put his hands behind his back, and, naturally, he smashed his head. I, my dear Signor Fifi, am putting my hands in front. I am putting them in front because my head, Signor Fifi, my head I want to

keep whole, healthy—and clear.
FIFI: But forgive me, if you don't know yet what my sister wants from you, why are you already thinking of how to save yourself?
CIAMPA: I close down the serious spring and reopen the social. (*Bowing.*) I am at your command.
BEATRICE: You must leave tonight for Palermo.
CIAMPA: For Palermo? And how? The president arrives tomorrow . . .
BEATRICE: Will the president have so much need of you at the bank tomorrow?
CIAMPA: Of course, pardon me . . . If he has no need of me, why does he hire me?
BEATRICE: I know that you keep the key to the strong box and that you stand around waiting for orders.
CIAMPA: You think that's all? You wish to humiliate me. I am a clerk, Signora.
FIFI: Don't you see that he has a pen behind his ear?
CIAMPA: Behind my ear, yes Signor. As a symbol. Doesn't the tavern have a bottle and a jug on its sign? I, a clerk, have my pen.
FIFI: Clerks and journalists!
CIAMPA: Leave the journalists be! A superfluous activity, that only flourishes at night. I write what the president tells me to write; I keep a register, Signora, of all the affairs of the bank. Did you think perhaps that all we do at the bank is sit and tell each other jokes? Or that I am there only for appearance? Has your husband had any occasion to complain of me?
BEATRICE: What? My husband? Of you? Just imagine it! May his tongue be cut out who would say such a thing!
CIAMPA: And you wish to send me this evening to Palermo?
FIFI: Why not? I don't see anything wrong with it.
BEATRICE: I will tell my husband that I sent you! Do you think he wouldn't give me permission to ask you a favor?
CIAMPA: A favor? But you may command me, Signora! You are the master! And as for me, my dear Signor Fifi, to take a breath of air in a great city such as Palermo is to live for a little while! I am suffocating here! Here I cannot breathe. But the moment I step out into the streets of a city I no longer seem to be walking on the earth; I'm in paradise! Ideas come to me! The blood rushes through my veins! If only I had been born there or in some city on the mainland, God only knows what I might have been now . . .
FIFI: A professor . . . A deputy . . . Perhaps even a cabinet minister!
CIAMPA: Why not king? But let's not exaggerate. We are puppets, my dear Signor Fifi! The Divine Spirit enters into us and pulls the strings. I am a puppet, you are a puppet, we are all puppets. Is it enough, do you think, to be born a puppet by divine will? No, Signor! Each can make himself the

puppet he wants, the puppet he can be or that he believes himself to be. And this is where all the insanity begins, Signora! Because each puppet wishes to be respected, not only for what he has inside himself, but for the mask he wears to the world. Not one of the puppets is contented with his role, each would like to stand before his own puppet and spit in its face. For example: you, Signora, are a wife, no?

BEATRICE: Yes, of course, at least . . .

CIAMPA: It is easy to see from the way you answer that you are not content. Because, whether you are a wife or not, you still wish to keep your respect, eh?

BEATRICE: Wish it? More! I demand it! And woe unto him who forgets it!

CIAMPA: There, you see? What did I say? And everyone is the same! The war here is between two puppets: the husband-puppet and the wife-puppet. Within, hair is torn, the truth is thrown wildly about the house. Outside, however, we wind, we wind, we wind the social spring here, the social spring there, the social spring everywhere, we smile, we bow, we shake hands—and the two puppets are happy, a triumph of pride and of sodden satisfaction.

FIFI: (*Laughing.*) You are really amusing yourself today, my dear Ciampa!

CIAMPA: But this is life, Signor Fifi! To keep the respect of everyone, Signora! To hold your puppet high—no matter what it looks like—so we may all keep our hair intact. I don't know if I have explained myself well enough. Let's return to the business at hand—what am I to do at Palermo?

BEATRICE: (*Who is far away, thinking.*) At Palermo?

FIFI: (*Snapping his fingers.*) Beatrice!

BEATRICE: Oh yes, that . . . I thought I heard Fana returning . . .

CIAMPA: Has the Signora by any chance changed her mind?

BEATRICE: I've changed nothing! (*To Fifi.*) Now where did I put that money?

FIFI: There, my darling sister, on the table.

BEATRICE: Ah yes, there it is. Here, Ciampa, here is 350 lire. (*Hands it to him.*)

CIAMPA: And what am I to do with it?

BEATRICE: Wait a moment. I'm going to get 150 lire more and two tickets.

CIAMPA: (*Looking at Fifi severely.*) Pawn tickets?

FIFI: Exactly. Why are you looking at me that way?

CIAMPA: Me? No, no! I am at your command!

BEATRICE: You're to get the objects out of hock. A pair of earrings and a bracelet. I'll get you the tickets. (*She goes out by the center door.*)

FIFI: My sister pawned the jewels to do me a favor. Her husband knows nothing about it . . .

CIAMPA: But good Lord, Signor Fifi, I am his employee . . .

FIFI: Don't worry, I'll tell him. I've returned the money. My sister wishes to have the object tomorrow.

CIAMPA: Tomorrow? Why tomorrow? What excuse will she find to tell the president for having sent me to Palermo on the very day he returns from his trip?

FIFI: I never knew a woman yet who couldn't find some excuse for anything.

CIAMPA: But the President has been gone for so long! Couldn't she have sent me several days ago? And no one would have been the wiser!

FIFI: I just returned the money today.

CIAMPA: Signor Fifi, there's a cat in the stew. Your sister has some idea behind all this.

FIFI: Yes, I must admit I've had the same thought. But what are you going to do? It's jealousy!

CIAMPA: And she sends *me* to Palermo?

(Beatrice returns, looking as if she had just had a violent argument.)

BEATRICE: Uh, here I am again . . . here I am.

FIFI: What happened?

BEATRICE: *(Making an effort to calm down.)* What happened?

FIFI: You seem so, so . . . I'm not sure.

BEATRICE: It's nothing. I couldn't find the tickets and I got annoyed. *(Giving them to Ciampa.)* Here they are. And here are the other 150 lire.

CIAMPA: Very well. But have you thought of what you're going to say to the president tomorrow when he comes to the bank and finds me gone? Have you thought of that?

BEATRICE: I've thought of everything! *(She shows in her other hand more money.)* See? This is for the trip, and here is another 150 lire.

FIFI: My, my, all those 100 lire bills . . .

CIAMPA: Yes, Signor Fifi. All these 100 lire bills . . .

BEATRICE: So? What of it? Have you finished making observations? *(To her brother.)* It's my own money, from what I've saved. *(To Ciampa.)* And you . . . all these 100 lire bills . . . Go on. Continue.

CIAMPA: Nothing, Signora. I would only say that you like to pull puppet strings, and to send the puppet to Palermo.

BEATRICE: Do you think I'm doing it *for my pleasure*? You know perfectly well why I'm sending you to Palermo. Now, with that other 150 lire—this *will* be for my pleasure—I want you to buy me a beautiful necklace, eh? With pendants.

CIAMPA: *(Astonished.)* A necklace?

BEATRICE: With pendants! I'll say to my husband that I saw *a certain friend of mine* wearing such a necklace and I liked it so much that I couldn't resist buying one. A caprice! My husband knows me.

CIAMPA: But Signora, excuse me, what do I know about these things?

BEATRICE: *(Annoyed.)* It doesn't matter. In that case, when you return you will tell me that you couldn't find it.

CIAMPA: Then why do you give me the money?

BEATRICE: Because it would give me so much pleasure if you did buy it. I want the *same thing* and *bought by you*, my dear Ciampa.

CIAMPA: Why by me? What do you want from me today, Signora? The *same thing*? How can I get the *same thing* when I don't even know what it looks like?

BEATRICE: I'll tell you. Go to Mercurio, our jeweller. *I know that my friend's necklace was bought from him*! Go there and you'll find the same thing. Isn't it about time you were off?

CIAMPA: Signora, I'm half stupefied. Half? What am I saying, half! Completely!

FIFI: It seems to me that she's found a good excuse for you!

BEATRICE: I'm preparing a delightful surprise for my husband! When he sees me tomorrow with the necklace around my neck . . . There's a train leaving at six, Ciampa.

FIFI: (*Looking at his watch.*) You have about an hour.

CIAMPA: Two minutes are enough for me. I must go and close up the bank. I'll place the bolt and then the chain on my door and then I'm off. I hope that the Signora will make good use of this hour.

BEATRICE: What do you mean?

CIAMPA: If the Signora would be good enough to think a bit, to reflect . . .

BEATRICE: What the devil am I going to think about?

FIFI: Let's go, Ciampa. I'll walk along with you. Goodbye, Beatrice.

BEATRICE: Goodbye, goodbye!

CIAMPA: Signora, I remind you of the case of my father, who put his hands behind his back . . .

BEATRICE: So?

CIAMPA: I'm going. I kiss your hand. (*Arriving at the door, he turns back.*) Signora, would you mind if I brought my wife here?

BEATRICE: Your wife? Here? That's all that's needed! You're a clown, Ciampa.

CIAMPA: (*Serious.*) For my peace of mind, Signora.

BEATRICE: Come now! Are you mad? What would we do here, with your wife?

CIAMPA: Nothing, of course; a great lady such as you . . . But only for my peace of mind.

BEATRICE: But if she's shut up, as you said, according to principle! Aren't you going to put up the bar?

CIAMPA: And the chain, Signora. And I'll bring you the key!

BEATRICE: What are you saying? I don't want it! Take the key with you!

CIAMPA: Ah, no! If the Signora does not wish my wife here, at least I must bring you the key! That's final!

BEATRICE: All right, all right, bring it; don't lose any more time!

CIAMPA: Let's go, Signor Fifi. (*They start to leave again. Ciampa turns back.*) You said with pendants, didn't you?
BEATRICE: Auff! Yes, with pendants.
CIAMPA: I kiss your hands, Signora. (*He leaves with Fifi La Belle. Beatrice runs to the door stage right.*)
BEATRICE: Commissioner, come in, come in here . . . At last!

(*Spano enters. A comic type of provincial Commissioner, bearded, heroic airs, steeped in his own world.*)

SPANO: Astonished, madam, thunderstruck! I swear it! Who could have guessed? Who would have known? Where's God in all this? What's He doing?
BEATRICE: All right, all right, but we have very little time, Commissioner. We must agree at once about what's to be done. Can you imagine, can you conceive of the fact that Ciampa wanted to bring his wife here?
SPANO: He? Here? His wife?
BEATRICE: What better proof do you want? What are we going to come to?
SPANO: Calm, Signora, be calm, for the love of God!
BEATRICE: How can I be calm? I'm going to give my husband a lesson before the entire country, a lesson he won't forget soon!
SPANO: Yes, but . . . the . . . the consequences, Signora? The consequences, have you thought of them?
BEATRICE: Of the separation, you mean? Of course I have. What do you think? But none of your "amicable separations," mind you. First the shame and then the separation. So no one will be able to say it was my fault! I want a scandal, and a big one! The people around here are going to see just what this man is that they all respect so much! I'll sign the denunciation. You're a public official and you can't refuse.
SPANO: Of course . . . Signora, of course . . . If you make out the denunciation . . .
BEATRICE: All right, let's do it quickly. Tell me how it's done.
SPANO: Ahahah, no! Pardon me, that I won't do! You want me, *me*, to write it for you?
BEATRICE: (*Angry.*) You won't help me? Commissioner . . . You don't want to help me?
SPANO: But of course, Signora! I want to help you . . . But think a bit . . . a friend of the family such as I am . . .
BEATRICE: It's your duty to do justice!
SPANO: Yes, Signora, and if I say so myself there's no one with a better sense of his duty than myself—I always walk thus, Signora, thus, with my head high, even before the Eternal Judge! But for the veneration that I have for the memory of your sainted father, who was a father to me also, Signora! Good Lord, the things he did for me! The things he taught me! Do you see,

Signora? Take care, walk softly, these . . . these little venial sins . . .
BEATRICE: Venial? You call them venial?
SPANO: One might even call them diversions. I speak now as a friend . . .
BEATRICE: As his friend?
SPANO: No, yours, Signora, above all yours!
BEATRICE: Diversions!! Oh, what lovely, lovely diversions! This is your justice? This is the way you help a poor woman who cannot defend herself? I want to write the denunciation, do you hear? Right now! Right now! How do I do it?
SPANO: Oh, great heavens, as for the denunciations, there's nothing simpler . . . It's the investigation, Signora, the investigation! Do you think that that's simple? A very delicate matter, extremely difficult . . . I must approach them, unseen . . . study the topography . . . Where does it all stop? Clues . . . Proofs . . .
BEATRICE: Everything's settled, everything's proven: nothing more is necessary, Commissioner! Do you know La Saracena?
SPANO: One of our informants, Signora.
BEATRICE: So much the better. Call her here! She knows everything, clues, proofs, and all.
SPANO: Signora, I've already spoken to her! But how's it to be done? There are but two ways to get in . . . one into the bank and one into Ciampa's apartment . . . But between the two there's a communicating door, right? This door Ciampa bars with lock and chain, yes or no? So what happens? I go there with the carabinieri, I knock and call out, "open in the name of the law." And then? Very simple. They separate. Your husband goes back into the bank through the communicating door, we enter, Signora Ciampa is in her room and your husband is at his desk.
BEATRICE: What's to be done? What's to be done? Is there no solution?
SPANO: No solution? But exactly here is where the art of the policeman comes into play, Signora. To find a solution! If you, for example, had a key to the bank . . .
BEATRICE: I have, I have! Ciampa's bringing me one himself before he leaves. I'm waiting for him now.
SPANO: Ciampa? How's that! Ciampa's bringing you the key?
BEATRICE: Yes, and I didn't even ask him for it! He insisted on bringing it here. I didn't want him to, but he wouldn't hear of anything else.
SPANO: I don't understand! No, I absolutely don't understand a thing! But now, now you can be absolutely sure that Ciampa suspects nothing, without the shadow of a doubt! Positive!
BEATRICE: What are you saying? And why would he want to bring his wife here, otherwise?
SPANO: Because . . . because . . . good Lord, because everyone knows, Signora; that is, it's a notorious fact . . .

BEATRICE: That I'm jealous, eh? And with that excuse, that I'm supposedly jealous, my husband does whatever he wants to. But I'll demonstrate very soon to all the world whether I'm right or wrong! So, now you know you'll have the key—everything's all right, eh? You open the door to the bank and . . .

SPANO: *(Smiling pityingly.)* I open? Open? Listen to her, "open!" Do you think the gentleman is so stupid that he goes into the woman's room without doing more than locking the door to the bank? No, he'll put the bar back into place, and the chain. Then what do I open? How do I open? We'll have to break it down. Art, Signora, the art of the policeman. In the meantime your husband has all the time necessary to arrange himself so as not to be caught in *flagrante delicto*. Things aren't done that way, Signora. If only it was that easy to be a commissioner!

BEATRICE: Oh God! Then how is it done?

SPANO: How is it done? . . . Hmmm . . . How is it done . . . Look! The president arrives at ten, eh? Now, at nine-thirty, I and one of my men hide ourselves in the cabinet behind the mimeograph machine—poof! We catch them! Poof! On the wing!

BEATRICE: *(Exultant.)* Ah! Bravo! Bravo! Now, the denunciation, quickly! *(The doorbell sounds.)*

SPANO: It seems to me someone rang.

BEATRICE: Yes, it must be Ciampa bringing me the key! Quickly, hide in here, it won't be a minute . . . *(She indicates a door stage right.)*

SPANO: On the wing! Do you understand?

(He leaves by the door, right. Ciampa opens the door center and looks in. He has with him a valise.)

CIAMPA: May I come in?

BEATRICE: Come in, come in, Ciampa. *(Suddenly she sees that following Ciampa is his wife.)* What's this?

CIAMPA: Signora, I have brought you my wife.

BEATRICE: *(Furious.)* Then take her back again, this minute!

CIAMPA: One word, Signora.

BEATRICE: I don't want to hear it! Leave, leave now! Can't you understand? I won't have her here.

CIAMPA: Signora, my wife is clean, modest . . .

BEATRICE: Oh, she's very clean, yes, I'm sure. . . ! And modest! Oh yes! *(Turning to Nina.)* I'm absolutely astonished that knowing as you do that you . . . you . . . have nothing to do here, that you should have come with your husband.

NINA: *(A woman of about thirty, more striking than modest, dressed almost like a lady, with great taste and cleanliness, rings, earrings. She answers with lowered eyes, but in a clear voice.*) Signora, if my husband has ordered me . . .

CIAMPA: (*Exultant.*) Marvelous!

BEATRICE: You could have saved yourself such touching obedience, since I absolutely forbade your husband to bring you here!

NINA: (*With her eyes lowered, but in a clear voice.*) I couldn't have known that, Signora!

CIAMPA: Superb!

BEATRICE: You've learned you part well, eh?

CIAMPA: No, Signora, she is telling the truth—quietly, modestly, as is proper. I took upon myself the responsibility of bringing her here. You won't take her?

BEATRICE: I've told you and I've told you that I don't want her here!

CIAMPA: You could keep her in the kitchen, or in the coal cellar, or she could even sleep under the stove with the cat.

BEATRICE: Do you want me to lose patience with you? Do you want me to say things that I must not say and don't want to say?

CIAMPA: Say them! Yes, say them, say them, Signora! I beg you to say them!

BEATRICE: I say get out, and that's all!

CIAMPA: So, you don't want her—very good—I've brought her here and you won't take her—excellent. And now, here is the key. I'm leaving. Remember, Signora, that I leave everything in your hands. (*He gives her the keys, then he winds up the social spring in the center of Nina's forehead and pretends to manipulate her like a puppet.*) Nina, wait. The social spring. A little bow, with eyes lowered, and then straight back to the house!

NINA: (*Bowing slightly.*) Your servant.

CIAMPA: Perfect! (*Nina leaves and Ciampa follows. At the door he turns and makes the gesture of winding the serious spring on the right.*) If the Signora would care to open . . .

BEATRICE: I'm opening nothing!

CIAMPA: Good! Then keep everything tightly shut!

CURTAIN

ACT II

The same, the next day. Beatrice, her hair in disorder and looking like a fury, shouts to Fana, who is off left.

BEATRICE: It doesn't matter! Hurry up, bring whatever there is! Whatever you've got! I want to be out of here by evening! Do you hear me? Out of this house! (*There is a knocking at the door.*)
FANA: (*Coming from the left door, her arms full of linen.*) Oh Mother of God, who could that be?
BEATRICE: Go and open it. If it's the commissioner, let him in and ask him to wait a moment. I can't receive him like this!

(*She goes out right. Fana goes to the door up center, puffing under her load. A moment later we hear a cry and Assunta La Bella, mother of Beatrice, and Fifi La Bella enter. The latter has Fana by the arm and is shaking her furiously. Both of them are very upset.*)

ASSUNTA: (*Running across the stage from the right door to the left, shouting.*) Beatrice! Beatrice! Where is she? Where is she? Beatrice! (*She goes out left, still shouting.*)
FANA: (*Defending herself from Fifi.*) Why are you shaking me, Signorino?
FIFI: (*Who still has her by the arm and is shaking her furiously.*) Because your duty was to come to me at once, to warn me!
ASSUNTA: (*Re-entering from the left.*) Where is my daughter? Tell me where she

is! Beatrice! Beatrice!
BEATRICE: (*Running through the door, right, and falling into her mother's arms.*) Mama! Mama! (*Bursts into tears.*)
ASSUNTA: My daughter, my daughter, what have you done? You're ruined!
FANA: (*Still trying to shake off Fifi.*) She insisted on doing everything herself, without telling anyone! I said to her so many, many times, I said, go to your brother, who is a man! Ask advice of your mamma before doing this!
ASSUNTA: Not to tell me, your mother! To go down to ruin like this, without telling a soul!
FIFI: (*Taking Beatrice by the arm and pulling her away from Assunta.*) It's too late to cry now! Do you know that you've got the whole province bubbling?
ASSUNTA: They've arrested them, Beatrice! They've arrested them!
FANA: The master? Great God!
ASSUNTA: And even her!
FANA: Even Ciampa's wife?
BEATRICE: Both of them? Wonderful! Now I'm happy! That's just what I wanted!
ASSUNTA: What are you saying?
FIFI: The shame? The scandal?
BEATRICE: Yes, fine, the scandal! The shame is on his head!
FIFI: And on yours! What did you think you were going to get from all this folly?
BEATRICE: What? Why this, this! (*She takes a deep breath and lets it out.*) Ah!—now I can breathe . . . like this! And I've given him a lesson he deserved!—I'm free! I'm free!
FIFI: Free? You're mad! What do you mean, free? Free to come home now, and never put your nose outside the door again! Free, she says! That's the end . . .
BEATRICE: I don't care about all that! I'm packing up now—why don't you help me instead of standing around shouting?
FIFI: Oh yes, I'll help you! Tell me something: was it that witch I saw you with yesterday?
FANA: Yes, yes, she's the one, Signorino!
ASSUNTA: Who's the one?
FANA: La Saracena, Signora.
ASSUNTA: Oh God, you're mixed up with that great pig? And you, Fifi, didn't you suspect anything?
FIFI: How could I have imagined this?
FANA: She sent me to bring Commissioner Spano . . .
FIFI: Spano?
ASSUNTA: Spano? How is it possible?
FIFI: What did he say?
ASSUNTA: (*To Beatrice.*) Spano, whom your father made, helped you to do this?

Without trying to dissuade you? When, when has such shame ever fallen upon the women of our family?
FANA: (*To Assunta.*) Your prudence and modesty, Signora mia, have always been the byword of the town!
ASSUNTA: How can it be, Fana? Can you tell me?
FANA: The new generation, Signora mia, the new generation!
ASSUNTA: How is it that you didn't have a thought for me, Beatrice? I'm old now! Do you think I can withstand such blows? Tomorrow I'll be dead . . . God only knows what I'm going through!
FIFI: Calm down, mother, calm down, for the love of God, or I don't know what I'll do! She wanted to get into this mess, now let her wallow in it!
ASSUNTA: Oh Lord, what are you saying? As if she were no longer my daughter and your sister! How can you?
FIFI: Is she still my sister? What more can we do about all this? The only thing we can do now is take her back home, because if there's one thing certain, it's that she can't stay with her husband!
BEATRICE: And who wants to stay?

(*The doorbell rings. They all stop as if suspended.*)

ASSUNTA: Who could it be?
BEATRICE: I'm not afraid of anyone!
FIFI: (*To Fana.*) Go and open it. Don't worry, I'm here.
FANA: (*To Fifi.*) Come with me, please, Signorino, I'm trembling . . .
FIFI: (*To Beatrice and Assunta.*) You two, leave the room. (*To Fana.*) Go on and open it! And stop making faces!
ASSUNTA: Come along, come along, my daughter, come with me . . . (*She leaves, right, with Beatrice.*)
FIFI: (*After Fana opens the door.*) Ah, it's you Commissioner!
SPANO: (*Entering.*) Always at your service, Signor Fifi.
FIFI: Oh yes, a lovely service you've done us, a wonderful service! You've given us every motive to thank you and consider ourselves in your debt.
SPANO: You wound me, Signor Fifi.
FIFI: But what sort of way is this, if you'll pardon me, to act towards a family which has always considered you a friend, and to which you owe so much?
SPANO: That's exactly why you wound me! In my innermost soul you wound me! I am a public official, Signor Fifi.
FIFI: Thanks very much, I know that. I'm talking to the friend! I don't understand it. You came here . . .
SPANO: . . . called by the Signora . . .
FIFI: . . . all right; and you received the denunciation?
SPANO: Did I receive the denunciation? What's that? Wait . . . You wound me, my dear Signor Fifi . . . First I did everything . . . the Signora . . .

Where is she?—Where is she?—She can tell you . . . I did everything, Signor Fifi, to persuade the Signora . . .
FIFI: You should have come to me first!
SPANO: With the denunciation already signed?
FIFI: I would have made her withdraw it!
SPANO: In that case I tell you that you don't know your sister! Good Lord, she would have gone straight to the inspector of police at Palermo saying that I . . . Ah, there she is, there she is!! (*Assunta and Beatrice re-enter from the right. Spano runs to kiss Signora Assunta's hand, but she withdraws it.*) Most respected Signora, no, please . . . let me, let me kiss your sainted hand . . . And you, Signora Beatrice, I beg you, tell your brother . . .
ASSUNTA: (*Interrupting him.*) It strikes me as being useless, Commissioner; useless, my dear Fifi, to go on with this farce.
BEATRICE: As for the rest, the commissioner is right.
SPANO: (*To Fifi.*) You hear?
BEATRICE: It was I, I alone, who did it.
SPANO: (*To Fifi.*) You hear? Oh blessed voice of truth! If I have any blame, dear, dear, Signor Fifi, blessed Signora Assunta . . . I venerate you, I swear, like a mother. You see? You've made me weep, Signor Fifi . . . Weep, you see, for if I have any blame it is precisely because of an excess of friendship! Don't you see? It's this damned profession (excuse the word) which when practiced in one's native town is the worst there can be!—But forgive me, forgive me, I should have done it all myself. I should have taken everything in hand, I should have gone to see Signor Fiorica. And what did I do? Through excess of friendship I've committed the worst of barbarities! This, this, Signor Fifi, is what you should reprove me for!
FIFI: But what did you do? What the devil? What did you do? Tell me!
SPANO: It's only that . . . I couldn't . . . I didn't want to do it myself . . . such a thing . . . I . . . entrusted the business to another . . . my colleague Logatto, a foreigner, Calabrese . . . And you see? You see what things he did? The fool! Donkey-head!
FIFI: He arrested them both, my brother-in-law and the lady?
BEATRICE: He did his duty, it seems to me! He did just exactly what he should have done!
ASSUNTA: Be quiet, daughter! You don't know what you're saying!
FIFI: He found them together. Tell me!
SPANO: Well . . . T-t-t-together, and not together. There was no *flagrante delicto*. This is all too much, really too much. From the state they were in . . . you understand . . . nothing can be proved, absolutely nothing!
FIFI: And so? Then why were they arrested?
SPANO: Why? Why, because I wasn't there! Because of that donkey-head of a Calabrese! This was my fault! But the president will be released, Signor Fifi, he'll be released this very evening. I promise and I swear! If not, my

name is no longer Alfio Spano!
FIFI: Very good, but tell me what happened!
SPANO: Oh yes, that. It was like this. Logatto, with the key I got from Signora Beatrice, entered the bank and hid himself in the old closet. When the carabinieri knocked on the door, demanding entrance in the name of the law, the president, while the lady came to open the door, naturally, what would he do? He tried to re-enter his office . . .
BEATRICE: (*With a triumphal cry.*) There, you see? So he was in Ciampa's apartment! He had opened the middle door!
SPANO: Yes, Signora . . .
BEATRICE: And how could he have opened it, if Ciampa had locked it and brought me the key? There's your proof! The real proof!
SPANO: No Signora, wait a moment, that's not proof . . .
BEATRICE: What do you mean, that's not proof?
SPANO: Let me speak. An English lock, Signora: there were two keys.
BEATRICE: Excellent! Two keys! One for Ciampa, and one for my husband!
SPANO: No Signora. Let me speak. The verbal deposition. The Cavaliere Fiorica has declared as follows: "Arriving at Catania, not being able to imagine why Ciampa was not there to greet me, being covered with dust from the journey—(poor gentleman), but wanting to read the correspondence which had arrived while I was away—(these are the words of the declaration), I knocked at the door to ask Ciampa's wife for something with which to wash my hands."
BEATRICE: (*Laughing stridently.*) His hands . . . Oh, marvelous . . . his hands . . . imagine!
SPANO: His hands, poor man! He had to open the letters . . .
FIFI: Never mind her! Go on.
SPANO: So then she, Ciampa's wife, he says, passed him, he says *the other key* under the door!
BEATRICE: Oh no, under the door! Oh, that's wonderful!
SPANO: (*Continuing.*) As I verified, Signora, the key does pass easily under the door. And the President was in his shirtsleeves, as decent as you wish.
BEATRICE: Yes? And she? How was she? Eh?
SPANO: She was . . . That is . . . She was . . .
BEATRICE: Say it! It must be in the declaration!
SPANO: I can say that she was not in her chemise . . .
BEATRICE: Naked? She was naked?
SPANO: No! What are you thinking of, Signora? What I'm trying to say is that she had more on than her chemise, as women wear around the house . . . what I mean is, women of the social rank, in this heat, I myself . . . my God, I'm sweating from head to foot . . . More than a chemise, Signora . . . She had on a skirt, a light skirt . . . Her arms were bare, it's true . . .
BEATRICE: So! Just because they weren't both found completely naked . . .

ASSUNTA: Beatrice! How can you say these things? I don't recognize you any more!
FIFI: For shame! In front of a man! (*Pointing to Spano.*)
BEATRICE: This is a man?
ASSUNTA: What's that?
BEATRICE: Let's hide it! Let's hide it all! Everything will be fine! We'll push all the shame under the rug! The shame is to say it; to do it, that's nothing at all!
FIFI: I don't understand, Commissioner! If the deposition was negative, why were they arrested?
SPANO: Well . . . Uh . . . They arrested the woman for . . . for . . . excessive decolletage, you understand! The president, because . . . Think a bit . . . When they broke in, the poor gentleman was furious, apoplectic! If I had been there I would have overlooked it, even if he had slapped me, I wouldn't have felt it, out of friendship! But that idiot Calabrese went and arrested him for insulting a public official. But he'll be released, Signor Fifi—I promise it and I swear it. This very evening! And if Logatto doesn't like it, he knows what he can do!
FIFI: In other words, there was no proof of any kind?
SPANO: None whatever! Everything was searched, including his suitcase. Even the jacket he was wearing . . .
BEATRICE: Ah, even the jacket? The suitcase? And tell me something: didn't you by any chance find a certain necklace with pendants, which he had promised to bring her from Palermo?
FIFI: Aha, so that's why you insisted that Ciampa get you a necklac with pendants?
BEATRICE: Exactly. (*To Spano.*) Answer me: did you find it?
SPANO: Pardon me, Signora, but who told you about such a necklace? La Saracena?
FANA: She's the one, Commissioner, she's the one!
SPANO: I knew it! She even told me about it! It's all nonsense, Signora, all nonsense! The truth is that Ciampa's wife, annoyed at being the object of the neighbor's gossip because of all the rings she wears, bragged that one day she'd make them die of envy by appearing at her window looking like the Madonna, wearing a huge necklace, one of those with pendants, around her neck. That's all! Incidentally, do you know what we did find in the president's suitcase? A prayer book, such a gem! A tiny little thing, beautiful! Bound in ivory with gilded pages.
ASSUNTA: You see? It was for you!
SPANO: Wait, there was also a box of chocolate-covered pecans.
ASSUNTA: The ones you like so much!
FANA: I've always said it, she's treated like a queen!
FIFI: Wretched ingrate!

(*Beatrice, repentant and tearful, falls into her mother's arms.*)

SPANO: (*Pleased with the effect he's produced, to Fifi.*) It seems to me it would be prudent, Signor Fifi . . . if I'm successful, as I hope, in getting the president released tonight . . . it would be prudent that the Signora not be found in the house.
ASSUNTA: Yes, yes! Absolutely!
FIFI: We'll take her home with us!
SPANO: At least for a few days. The poor man has a devil in his head, and if he found her here there's no telling what he might do.
FIFI: And he's right! He's right! I don't know what *I'd* do in his place!
SPANO: It will pass, believe me, it will pass! After a few days his fury will evaporate and everything will return to normal.—Ah, great God, what a wonderful thing is domestic peace!

(*A long pause, as if everything were finished, settled. Suddenly, a violent banging on the door.*)

FANA: (*Jumping with fright.*) Oh, Lord help us! It's him. Ciampa!
FIFI: Great God, we'd forgotten all about Ciampa!
SPANO: Good Lord, with his wife in prison . . .
ASSUNTA: What will we do? What can we do for the poor man?
SPANO: It might be better not to receive him!
FIFI: No, it's better to receive him and try to reason with him!
SPANO: Yes . . . Maybe . . . I hope he doesn't do something crazy . . .
FIFI: Let him do what he wants to! After all, he has the right . . .
FANA: I'm trembling in every muscle!
BEATRICE: (*Humbly*) It might be better if Mama and I leave the room, eh?
FIFI: (*Glaring at her and shouting.*) I should think so!
ASSUNTA: Let's go, let's go, my daughter. Leave him with the men. (*They leave through the door, right.*)
FIFI: (*To Fana, who tries to leave with the other women.*) Where are *you* going? Go open the door!
SPANO: Don't be afraid, I'm here to protect you! (*Fana goes out into the vestibule and then re-enters, terrified.*)
FANA: Mother of God! He's dead! He's fallen and killed himself!
FIFI & SPANO: What? What happened?

(*They run out to help Ciampa. Ciampa enters, cadaverous, with his clothes and face smeared with mud, his forehead cut, his tie all awry and his glasses broken. Fifi and Spano hover about him, solicitous, wiping the dust off his coat with their hands.*)

FIFI: My dear Ciampa! What happened?

SPANO: Did you fall?
CIAMPA: (*Quietly, calmly.*) Nothing. An accident. A little accident. But my glasses are broken.
FIFI: (*Running to get a chair, while Spano and Fana get two others at the same time.*) Here, sit down . . . Sit down here . . .
SPANO: Here's a seat . . .
CIAMPA: Thank you. I won't sit.
FIFI: What? Why not?
CIAMPA: Because I won't.
SPANO: But your legs won't hold you!
CIAMPA: Don't worry. I have nine souls, like a cat . . . In any case I'll be leaving soon. Where is the Signora?
SPANO: The Signora, Ciampa, it seems to me . . . Well . . .
FIFI: You must understand that she can't speak to you now . . .
CIAMPA: Speak? What need is there for talk? What's done is done.
FIFI: Yes, but it's not as you think . . .
SPANO: Negative! The deposition was absolutely negative!
FIFI: There, you hear? You hear what the commissioner said? You have no reason to feel this way, I assure you.
CIAMPA: You assure me?
SPANO: No, no! The declaration! The declaration! The deposition, you understand, my dear Ciampa? The deposition says it!
FIFI: Of course! The whole thing was completely unfounded!
SPANO: Le-gal-ly un-found-ed!
FIFI: Everything's finished, settled!
CIAMPA: Fine, fine. I have something to give to the Signora.
FIFI: The things you got in Palermo? You can give them to me.
CIAMPA: Fine, fine.—However, it seems to me better, since the commissioner is here, to give them to him.
FIFI: Certainly, to him or to me. (*To Spano.*) A few little things Ciampa got back from the pawnbrokers . . .
SPANO: Of course, of course.
FIFI: (*To Ciampa.*) You can leave them there, if you like . . . (*Indicating the little table.*)
CIAMPA: You give so much weight to the formality of a deposition?
FIFI: A deposition is a statement of facts! As the commissioner said . . .
SPANO: Precisely, all legal!
CIAMPA: Very good! I want the deposition to show, also, another fact: That I gave to the commissioner these objects, which the Signora sent me . . .
SPANO: Yes, yes, I know, my dear Ciampa!
CIAMPA: You know? *Sent away on this errand.* And it must state the fact that I, as a humble servant, left and came back after performing the errand, and turned over to you these two objects. (*Takes the two small boxes from his pocket.*)

One . . . two . . . That's all. (*He starts to leave.*)
FIFI: What are you going to do?
CIAMPA: Nothing. I'm leaving.
FIFI: You're leaving like that?
CIAMPA: What do you want me to do? I wished to speak to the Signora. I can't. I'm going.
FIFI: If you'll pardon me, could I know what you want to say to my sister? (*Fana, in the background, motions "no, no" to Fifi. Ciampa, turning, sees her.*)
CIAMPA: You have a sore throat, perhaps? Difficulty with your breathing? By your rules I'd lie on the ground and count the stars, even without glasses! (*To Fifi.*) Is she afraid if I talk to your sister . . .
FIFI: (*Interrupting.*) Why should she be afraid? It's just that it would be best not to see her just now. I, Commissioner Spano, and my mother, who is with her now, we've made her see her folly in all this, and she's very upset. Penitent, that's the word, she's extremely penitent. Isn't that right?
SPANO: The devil! She's crying!
CIAMPA: Ah, she's crying . . .
FIFI: She's crying, she's crying, because—the commissioner and I—we painted the whole matter in very black colors . . .
SPANO: It's true . . . blacker than black!
FIFI: I assure you, Ciampa, that you couldn't say anything that I haven't already said!
CIAMPA: What do you imagine? What do you think I would say to a lady? Your sister has done nothing more than take my name—my puppet . . . Do you remember me speaking yesterday about puppets?—my puppet: throw it to the ground and then—a little kick—like this! (*He throws his cap on the ground and kicks it.*) Because the Signora—poor little puppet—believed herself wronged . . . Our position—mine and hers—at bottom they're the same: she there, I here . . . What could I say to her? I simply want to ask her a question; and not really to her, but to her conscience.
FIFI: What question?
CIAMPA: Pardon me, only to her conscience . . . (*Suddenly turning to Spano.*) Commissioner, search me.
FIFI: No, no, what are you saying?
SPANO: We know that you're a gentleman, Ciampa!
CIAMPA: As for that, I am what I am. I'm glad you see me now, Commissioner, weeping, weeping tears of blood. Tears of blood because I have been murdered . . . (*He bursts into uncontrollable sobs.*)
FIFI & SPANO: No—No! What are you saying? But you're wrong, you're wrong! Calm yourself, Ciampa!
CIAMPA: Calm, yes. This question, in short, to the Signora, in your presence, will you let me ask it?
FIFI: Yes, yes, of course! I'll call her. (*Calling through the door right.*) Beatrice!

mamma! Come in, Beatrice! (*To Beatrice, who enters with her mother.*) Here's Ciampa, who wants to ask you a question.

ASSUNTA: (*With pity.*) Oh, my poor man, are you hurt?

CIAMPA: It's nothing, signora. The worst thing is that I've broken my glasses. I see and I don't see. But, in any case, there's nothing left to see. (*To Beatrice.*) One question only to you, Signora Beatrice: do you believe . . . leaving aside what happened this morning . . . do you believe, in conscience, that you were right in doing what you did, although I, in the presence of your brother . . .

ASSUNTA: (*Trying to interrupt him.*) Oh yes, we know everything, Ciampa!

FIFI: You even brought your wife here!

CIAMPA: Please . . . Please . . . Let her say it! It's possible that the signora, not withstanding everything else, wished to hurt me too, believing that she had every reason to do so. Is that it, Signora? Answer me—in conscience!

BEATRICE: (*Hesitantly.*) No . . . I . . . I . . .

SPANO: The Signora didn't want to hurt you, my dear Ciampa! So much so that she even sent you away, to Palermo!

BEATRICE: That's it . . . I . . . As the commissioner says . . .

CIAMPA: Ah, no Signora! That you did not think of me is not possible! Because for two hours, here in this room, I did nothing else but put my hands before me!

BEATRICE: Yes, yes. That's just why I sent you to Palermo! To be free to deal with your wife and my husband!

CIAMPA: Without a thought for me?

BEATRICE: Without a thought for you.

CIAMPA: And what was I? Nothing? A stone to whet yourself on? You threw me to the floor. You took me thus, between two fingers, like a dustcloth, you tossed me in a corner, as if no notice need be taken of me at all . . . I want to know everything, Signora! I want to enter into your conscience, descend to its very depths, and discover whether you had the tiniest scruple about hurting me, because I—according to you—knew everything and said nothing. Am I right? Answer me! Am I right?

BEATRICE: Well . . . You said it yourself . . . Yes, that's it exactly.

CIAMPA: Ah! So that if you see a lame man—let's say—you put a sign on him which says: "Look, everyone, he's crippled!"

BEATRICE: No, no . . . What a terrible thing . . .

CIAMPA: We'll leave the lame man to one side. Everyone can see that he's lame, without a sign. You must prove to me that *one person, one only,* in this whole province, suspected me of being what you believed me to be! That *one person, one only,* could come to me and say in my face: "Ciampa, you're a cuckold, and you know it."

FIFI: (*Quickly.*) No, no! No one!

SPANO: (*Simultaneously.*) Who could think such a thing?

ASSUNTA: (*Simultaneously.*) God in heaven, absolutely no one!

CIAMPA: (*Dominating the exclamations.*) But the Signora could say: If no one else knew it, you knew it, and that was enough!—Is that right? Is that right? Don't deny it! I need your conscience, signora, not a deposition! Say it: Is that right?

BEATRICE: Yes, that's right.

(*A movement of surprise and consternation among the others. Silence.*)

CIAMPA: (*Hurt, lowering his hand.*) Ah, Signora.—I'll speak now . . . Not for myself . . . I speak in general terms . . . How can you know, Signora, why this one robs, why that one kills. How can you know why another, let's say old, ugly, poor . . . loves a woman who has his heart fixed in a vise . . . who needs only to say "Come here," and press her mouth against his to make the poor old man drunk with joy—how can you know, Signora, with what pain, with what torture, this old man can finally bring himself to the point of sharing this love with another—rich, young, handsome—especially if the woman satisfies them both and is very careful to hide everything. I'm speaking in general, Signora . . . I'm not speaking of myself! And yet it's a wound, Signora, a terrible, festering wound! And what do you do? You stretch out your hand and rip it open, like this . . . Publicly! Let's leave this example and come back to ourselves. I, Signora, knew that you suspected my wife and your husband.—Jealousy!—Who has not known it, whether they want to or not?—I feel pity for the criminal, Signora, how is it that I would not feel pity for one who is jealous? I came here yesterday to make you talk! To make you speak out! You have suspicions? I can't cure them! With suspicions of this kind, the more you try to root them out the deeper they get! If you had spoken frankly with me, I would have returned home and said to my wife: "Pack up, we're leaving." Today I would have gone to the bank and said to the president: "Sir, I kiss your hands: I cannot stay any longer!" "Why, dear Ciampa?" "Because I cannot stay with you any longer: I have other things to do." That's how it's done, Signora! Why do you think I brought my wife, yesterday? To make you break out with the storm you had inside you! I even begged you, "Speak, speak!" But you didn't want to say anything! You wanted to throw me on the ground, to murder me . . . and what do I do now? Tell me what must I do now? Buy myself a pretty cap with two nice horns to make my appearance in public? To have all the children of the town follow me, shouting: "Beee . . . Beee . . ." And I, happy and smiling, bowing right and bowing left, and saying, "Thank you"?

FIFI: What are you saying? What cap? What horns? What children? Nothing happened!

SPANO: Nothing at all! Less than nothing!

CIAMPA: Because the declaration says so, eh? Tell me, who's going to believe the declaration after all this scandal? Carabinieri, commissioner, surprise arrest . . .

SPANO: Yes, but with negative results! That means . . .

CIAMPA: Signor Commissioner, these things are like oil stains, they never come off. They'll say "It's because he is an important man, they've arranged everything." And where does that leave me? You, Signora, you could have had the pleasure of giving your husband a little lesson, if it had been a matter of some girl without parents, without relatives. Everything would have been arranged. But there is someone else involved here, Signora. Now is it that you didn't think of me? Was I nothing? You've had your fun, the whole province is giggling, and tomorrow you'll make your peace with your husband. And I? For you it will be all finished—but me? I've got the declaration . . . negative. And tomorrow? Everyone will approach me, look me in the eyes and say, "It was nothing, Ciampa, the Signora was amusing herself!" (*Suddenly.*) Signor Commissioner, here, feel my pulse. (*He holds out his wrist.*)

SPANO: (*Astonished.*) What's that? Why?

CIAMPA: Feel my pulse. And tell me whether it is beating regularly or not. I say—with the greatest calm in the world—you are all my witnesses—that this evening, or tomorrow, when my wife returns to the house, I will split her head open with an axe! (*Suddenly.*) And I will not kill her alone, for that would merely give pleasure to the Signora, I must also kill him, the cavaliere. I'm forced to, I have no choice.

FIFI & SPANO: (*Grasping Ciampa, while the three women shout and weep.*) What's that? You're mad! Who are you going to kill?

CIAMPA: (*Pale, almost smiling.*) Both of them. I must! I can't do less! I didn't want it!

FIFI: You won't kill anyone, because there's no reason to! And even if there were, we're here to stop you!

SPANO: I'm here.

CIAMPA: Signor Commissioner, if you stop me today . . .

SPANO: And tomorrow!

CIAMPA: I'll do it day after tomorrow! Woe unto him who has murdered the heart of another! I'm calm, Signor Commissioner. I've told you I didn't want this. I didn't want it! But I can't remain as I am!

BEATRICE: But I've told you just now, Ciampa, I've told you that you have no reason . . .

CIAMPA: *Now* you've told me, eh, Signora? *Now.* You realize it *now*, that you shouldn't do a thing like this to any man? It's too late, Signora!

FIFI: But pardon me, if she realizes now, that it was nothing . . .

CIAMPA: That "nothing," Signor Fifi, you must not say that to me!

FIFI: It was madness, the whole thing, a moment of insanity!

ASSUNTA: (*Picking it up.*) Insanity, Ciampa! Madness!
SPANO: It was madness, the Signora admits it herself!
FIFI: She admits it! We all confirm it! Madness!
ALL: Yes, yes! Madness! Insanity!

(*In the midst of everyone shouting "Madness! Insanity!" Ciampa suddenly becomes radiant with an inner light.*)

CIAMPA: Oh God! How beautiful! How marvelous! Peacefully! Oh wonderful! Yes, yes, everything can be adjusted!!! Peacefully . . . Oh, I can breathe! I think I'll dance . . . jump . . . a tremendous weight's been taken off my back! My hands . . . My hands can remain clean, and I kiss them! I kiss them! You, Signora, get ready at once! At once!
BEATRICE: (*Astonished, as are they all.*) I? Why?
CIAMPA: Do what I say, go and prepare yourself! We must not lose time! (*Looks at his watch.*) You'll make it! You'll make it!
BEATRICE: What do you mean? Where am I going?
FIFI: What are you talking about?
SPANO: Where's the Signora supposed to go?
CIAMPA: Yes, yes! Don't you see? You, Fana, and you, Signora Assunta, go and help her put a few things in her suitcase! Quickly, for God's sake! There's no time to lose!
BEATRICE: No time to lose for what? Where am I going? Have you gone crazy?
CIAMPA: I? Gone crazy? No, pardon me, you're the one who's gone crazy! Your brother recognizes it, the commissioner recognizes it, your mamma, everyone! And therefore, you're crazy! If you're crazy, you must go to the insane asylum! It's simple!
FIFI: What? What?
ASSUNTA: My daughter? What are you saying?
BEATRICE: To the asylum? Me? To the asylum?
CIAMPA: Never mind the asylum! A sanatorium, let's say! Three months. A vacation.
BEATRICE: (*Indignant.*) You're the one who should go to an asylum! You! Get out! Get out of my house! Right now!
CIAMPA: Signora, where are you sending me? I beg you to understand that I'm speaking in your interest!
SPANO: But what are you suggesting we do, Ciampa?
FIFI: Where are we?
CIAMPA: Even you, Signor Fifi? Don't you see that this is the only way? For her! For the president! For everyone! Don't you see that she's made her husband ridiculous, and now she must make amends before the entire province? If you say: "She's *insane!*" everything's finished, everyone under-

stands! *Insane, she must be cared for and cured!* Only that way will I be freed from the necessity of vengeance! What can I say? *She's crazy, what does it matter what a madwoman says?* That's all! Tomorrow the president won't have to be mortified in front of his friends: and the signora will have three months of vacation!—Go on, go on, there's no better way! But you must leave this very evening!

FIFI: Yes, he's right! He's right! (*To Beatrice.*) Do you understand? You'll merely be pretending!

BEATRICE: But . . . But . . . You're mad! Go to an asylum? Do you hear them, mamma? To an asylum!

ASSUNTA: But it's all for the best, my daughter.

SPANO: For the best, Signora! It also seems to me the best solution! Think of your husband, Signora . . .

BEATRICE: You're crazy too! You want me to pass for a madwoman before the entire province?

CIAMPA: Before the entire province, Signora, you stamped three people with the mark of shame. One, as an adulterer; another, as a whore; and myself, as a cuckold. You wish to say that you have committed a folly? That's not enough, Signora! You must show yourself as being insane—really insane—enough to be cared for in an asylum!

BEATRICE: You're the one that should be cared for!

CIAMPA: No, Signora, you. For your own good. We all know now that you're insane. And now the whole province must know it. Don't worry, Signora! There's nothing simpler than being insane, believe me! I'll teach you how it's done. It's enough to tell everyone the truth. No one will believe you, and they'll all take you for a madwoman!

BEATRICE: (*Convulsed with fury.*) Ah, so you know that I was right, that I had the right to do what I did?

CIAMPA: No. Ah no! Turn the page, Signora! If you turn the page you'll read that there's nothing more insane in all the world than to believe that you are right!—Come now! Give yourself the pleasure of being mad for three months! You think it's nothing? To be insane? If only I could do it! (*Making appropriate gesture of winding insane spring.*) Think of it, Signora! To wind the insane spring as far as it will go! To put on the madman's cap and bells and run through the streets spitting the truth into the faces of the passersby! We're all suffocating, Signora! We're suffocating in the face of injustice, of pretense, of shame and greed; they make us sick to our stomachs! But we can't wind the insane spring! You can! Give thanks to God! Begin to shout!

BEATRICE: Begin to shout?

CIAMPA: Yes! In your brother's face! In the commissioner's face! Now! In *my* face! And be sure that only a madman can give himself the pleasure of shouting to my face: Beee!

BEATRICE: All right, cuckold, yes: Beee! . . . You see? I'm shouting in your

face, you see? Beee! Beee!
FIFI: (*Trying to restrain her.*) Beatrice!
SPANO: Signora!
ASSUNTA: Daughter!
BEATRICE: (*With an insane cry of fury.*) No! I'm crazy? Then I have to shout: Beee! Beee! Beee!
CIAMPA: (*As Beatrice continues to shout and the others try to restrain her.*) She's mad! She's insane! Here's the proof! Oh, how beautiful! She must be taken to the asylum! To the asylum!

(*He dances with delight, clapping his hands. A moment of great confusion, as the neighbors of the Fioricas begin to come in, whispering and talking to each other. Ciampa continues to clap his hands, radiant with joy, and answering their questions by saying:*)

CIAMPA: She's crazy! She's insane! They're taking her to the asylum! She's mad!

(*And as the neighbors surround the commissioner and the brother, whispering, softly, softly, about the terrible misfortune, Ciampa sits on a bench in the middle of the stage and bursts into a horrible laugh, of rage, of savage joy, and of desperation, all at the same time.*)

CURTAIN

MAN, BEAST AND VIRTUE

A Comedy

Translated by Roger W. Oliver

CHARACTERS

Rosaria, housekeeper
Toto, pharmacist
Paolino, schoolteacher
Giglio, student
Belli, student
Mrs. Perella, wife of Captain Perella
Nono, son of Captain and Mrs. Perella (age 11)
Dr. Puleio, physician
Grazia, serving woman
Sailor, subordinate of Captain Perella
Captain Perella, sea captain

The play takes place in an Italian seaport city, the name of which is not important, around 1920. Act I is set in the studio/reception area of Paolino's home. Act II is set, later the same day, in the dining room of the Perella home. Act III also occurs in the Perella dining room, at dawn of the next day.

ACT I

A modest room in Paolino's house which serves as studio and reception area. It is furnished with a desk, bookcases filled with books, a sofa, easy chairs, etc. The door to the kitchen is left. There is another exit to the right, with a third door at the rear which opens into an almost completely dark closet. When the lights go up the room is in chaos. Several chairs have been overturned on top of each other in the middle of the room. The easy chairs are in odd positions. Rosaria, the housekeeper, enters from the kitchen with her hair in curlers and covered by a hairnet. She has recently spread a horrible almost rose-colored pomade on her head. She resembles a stupid and petulant old hen. Toto follows her, hat in hand, wearing a collar reversed like a priest. He resembles a contrite fox. He continually rubs his hands under his chin, as if he were washing himself in the fountain of Rosaria's sweet, stupid grace.

ROSARIA: Will you tell me something? Why do you insist on showing up here every morning before I have a chance to get this place cleaned up? Does this look like a house that's ready to receive visitors—whether they've been invited or not?

TOTO: What can I say, Rosaria, my dear. As far as I'm concerned . . .

ROSARIA: (*With an outburst of temper, turning toward him as if she wanted to peck at him.*) What do you want?

TOTO: (*Awkwardly, with a vain smile.*) It makes no difference to me. I've got to go open my drugstore and I wanted to leave this key for my brother so the poor guy can pick it up here when he gets back from his night calls at the hospital.

ROSARIA: Fine, but why can't you just give me the key at the door, without coming in here?

TOTO: But I enjoy this little duty.

ROSARIA: You call it a duty. I call it a bad habit.

TOTO: You know, Rosaria, you're not very nice to me.

ROSARIA: I'm busy. I'm a very busy person. And on top of that you bore me. Take a look at this place—it's almost as much of a mess as I am. Chairs all over the place. A house—when it's an honest house—should be allowed to keep its modesty, just like a woman when *she's* honest.

TOTO: I agree with you completely. And it's so nice to hear you talk that way: a modest house . . . a modest woman . . .

ROSARIA: I'm so happy you agree. And yet you violate her.

TOTO: (*Horrified.*) Who? Me?

ROSARIA: This house! The modesty of this house. (*As she speaks she returns the chairs to their upright position and replaces the pieces of cloth that cover their legs. She does this with a grotesque modesty, as if she were concealing the legs of a young woman.*) God knows, this isn't the first time I've thought about this. I work for someone who . . . (*With her hand she makes a gesture of chagrin, indicating the door to the right.*) Agh, it's enough to make these chairs not only fall over but get up and rush off to get away from his screaming and yelling. If I were one of these chairs I'd rather be dragged through the streets than live here, where that ill-mannered lout could kick me, pick me up and shake me and then throw me around whenever he was angry.

TOTO: But you look after them. Like they were your own daughters.

ROSARIA: A chair should be neat and clean like a young bride. I look after myself . . . I look after them.

TOTO: Like a young bride . . . Ooh, to have a home, a real home!

ROSARIA: What are you talking about? What about your place next door? All you have to do is find someone to take care of it for you.

TOTO: No, what I mean, Rosaria, is a *home*, a real home, with a family.

ROSARIA: So get married. Or find a friendly housekeeper. Hey, that's not a bad idea. For you and your brother the doctor. You could share.

TOTO: (*Quickly, with horror.*) Oh, not with him! That would never work at all. I'm sure it would make *him* very happy, but he would never do it with me around.

ROSARIA: So you're a sort of substitute wife for your brother?

TOTO: No, no, not at all. I just look after everything, you see? So he doesn't need a thing. When he returns from the hospital, he'll come over here for the key and when he gets home he'll find everything in order, with all his needs taken care of . . .

ROSARIA: Lucky man!

TOTO: And I do it willingly, with all my heart. Believe me, my brother means the world to me. The home is for him . . . it's not for me.

ROSARIA: Is that why you spend all day cooped up in your drugstore . . .

TOTO: No, that's not the reason. Poor guy, even during the day he has to go out to see patients. No, a person's real home, Rosaria my dear, is never the home we make for ourselves, the one we take so much trouble with. Our real home, the one whose smell we evoke when we say the word "home" —a smell that as we recall it is both so sweet yet so full of pain—our real home is the one others made for us. I mean, of course, the one our dear father and mother made with their love and care. And even for them, our blessed parents, the home they created for us wasn't *their* true home; that was the one made for them by their parents, not by themselves. And so on—it's always the same. Oh, but here comes Paolino.

(*Paolino enters in a rush from the right. He's about thirty, very animated, but with a nervous energy that comes from intolerance. All passions, all the spiritual stirrings of the soul, become transparent in him, with an obviousness that trumpets attention to them. He is given to sudden outbursts and changes of mood and humor. He doesn't allow for the objections of others and he cuts them short.*)

PAOLINO: (*To Toto.*) Good morning, my dear friend. (*Suddenly turning to Rosaria.*) You haven't given him any coffee yet? Go get some, for God's sake. How long does he have to sing to you before he earns his morning cup of coffee?

TOTO: Paolino, please. That's not why I come over here.

PAOLINO: Toto, do me a favor. In addition to being a freeloader don't be a hypocrite too . . .

TOTO: I was just talking about . . .

PAOLINO: About the home. You went on for half an hour about the home. I heard you from in there: you were extolling the poetic nature of the home.

TOTO: But I really do feel that way.

PAOLINO: I'm not saying you don't. But it serves to hide your sponging behind a veil of decency.

TOTO: No . . .

PAOLINO: But isn't it true that as soon as Rosaria gives you some coffee you leave, rubbing your hands as you go down the stairs, very pleased with the little reward you manage to sponge off me every morning with your poetic babble?

TOTO: Well, if that's what you think of me! (*Mortified, about to leave.*)

PAOLINO: (*Grabs his arm.*) Where are you going? You came for your morning cup of coffee and by God you're going to get it. I only say all of this because it's true.

TOTO: No, it isn't.

PAOLINO: Yes, it is. And because it's true you must have some coffee!

TOTO: I won't drink it.
PAOLINO: (*Impetuously following this line.*) We'll make it two cups. No, three. Because you honestly believe that you've earned it for all that rhetoric you've dished up. Understand? When something gets me here (*indicates the pit of his stomach*) then I'm finished. I've told you. I'll pay up. A cup of coffee a day—you can count on it. Now get out of here. (*He acts as if the matter were settled, and when Toto moves toward him to pursue it further . . .*) No, no, just go. Don't try to thank me.
TOTO: I don't want to thank you. I would feel much better if you made me . . .
PAOLINO: (*With an angry outburst.*) Pay for it?
TOTO: (*With his usual humility.*) At the end of the month, like it was all my idea.
PAOLINO: What do you think this is—a cafe?
TOTO: Of course not. But what I drink here isn't made just for me. You have a charming housekeeper. She doesn't make coffee just to sell to me. Besides what she makes for the two of you, she makes an extra cup for me. And I'm willing to pay you for it.
PAOLINO: That's just great. Suppose I were married. It wouldn't be for your convenience, but for mine, all right. But then I let you have her only for five minutes or so every day. After all, what's five minutes?
TOTO: (*Smiling.*) That's not the point. A wife . . .
PAOLINO: (*At once.*) And a housekeeper?
TOTO: (*Not understanding.*) What?
PAOLINO: (*Shouting.*) Do you think that coffee can make itself? It takes a housekeeper to make coffee. Or maybe, you beast, you think that even a common laborer is better off than a teacher because the laborer can do everything by himself, while a teacher can't. He has to hire a housekeeper.
ROSARIA: (*Interrupting, mellifluous and persuasive.*) Everything I do in this house is for you . . .
PAOLINO: (*Understanding the bitterness of this honey, trying to suppress it.*) Let's drop the whole thing.
ROSARIA: (*Resentful, with implications of reproach.*) If there's no order in a home, everything falls apart.
PAOLINO: Thank you very much. (*To Toto.*) Do you hear that? Because I have the good luck of being a teacher, I have to suffer the consequences, while you, as a pharmacist, don't have to. What the hell! Rosaria, let him have some coffee today, then starting tomorrow, no more.
TOTO: Excuse me, but you've just insulted me. You called me a beast.
PAOLINO: So I did. Give him a cup tomorrow, too. Now please leave me alone. Or do you want me to pile on the insults so that you can get a free cup of coffee for every remark I make?
TOTO: That won't be necessary. I'm on my way. And thank you, Paolino. (*He exits left, with Rosaria.*)

PAOLINO: God, such people! Is the whole world like this?

GIGLIO: *(From offstage)* Excuse me, sir.

PAOLINO: Oof, my first students already. All right. Come in. *(Giglio and Belli enter, carrying books under their arms. Each wears a wool scarf around his neck, one red and the other blue. Each has a bestial aspect that puts one at ease—for Giglio it's a black billygoat, for Belli it's a monkey with glasses.)*

GIGLIO: Good morning, sir.

BELLI: Good morning, sir.

PAOLINO: Good morning, boys. Please sit down. *(Indicates the desk.)*

GIGLIO: *(As he sits.)* Thank you very much, sir.

BELLI: *(As he sits.)* Thank you very much, sir.

PAOLINO: *(Sits down himself and looks from one to the other, giving each a slight nod.)* Don't mention it, dear Giglio. Don't mention it, dear Belli. *(He snorts with exasperation.)* Ahhh! *(Putting his head in his hands.)* Oh, God, God, God, God, God. I really believe that very soon life on this planet will no longer be possible.

GIGLIO: Why is that, sir?

BELLI: Will you explain that to us, sir.

PAOLINO: *(Facing them, with suppressed rage.)* How old are the two of you?

GIGLIO: Eighteen, sir.

BELLI: Seventeen, sir.

PAOLINO: *(Shaking his head as he contemplates their bestial aspects.)* Then you're both almost men. Tell me: what's the word for actor in Greek?

GIGLIO: In Greek?

PAOLINO: No. In Arabic. You don't know. *(To Belli.)* What about you?

BELLI: Actor. . . ? I don't remember.

PAOLINO: Ah, you don't remember. That means you did know it once but now you can't recall it?

BELLI: N-, No, sir. I never knew it.

PAOLINO: Then say so! *I-don't-know.* I will teach it to you then. In Greek the word for actor is *hypocrites*. And why *hypocrites*? What do actors do?

BELLI: Well, they speak lines, I suppose.

PAOLINO: You suppose. You're not sure. And just because they speak lines, they're called hypocrites? Does it seem right to call someone who recites for a profession a hypocrite? If he's only doing his job, why should he be called a hypocrite? How would you describe, then, someone with the name that the Greeks gave to actors?

GIGLIO: *(His face lights up all of a sudden.)* Oh. Someone who pretends to be someone else.

PAOLINO: Exactly. Someone who pretends to be someone else. An actor plays a part, like that of a king, when he is really a poor beggar, or whatever else he might be. What's wrong with that? Nothing. It's a job, a profession. When does it become wrong? When someone isn't a hypocrite out of duty, as a job on the stage, but because he does it out of habit, or for profit, in real life. Or just to be polite—definitely then, since politeness means just that: seeming to be the exact opposite of what you really are. Gall tasting like honey. Or, when someone comes in here and says "Good morning, sir" when he really wants to say "Why don't you go to hell, sir."

GIGLIO: What? Pardon me.

BELLI: We should tell you to go to hell?

PAOLINO: It would be better, I assure you, far better. And best of all would be to say nothing. Nothing at all.

GIGLIO: But then you would tell us what bad manners we have.

PAOLINO: Precisely. Because politeness means that we wish a good day to the very people we would see go to hell. And to have good manners is exactly this—to be actors. *Quod Erat Demonstrandum*. Now, history today, correct?

BELLI: But, pardon me sir, listen . . .

PAOLINO: That's enough. The digression is over. This politeness, my boys, is giving me an ulcer. Enough about acting and manners. Now we'll do a little history. (*A knock is heard.*) Who is it? Come in.

ROSARIA: (*She enters from the kitchen and beckons to Paolino with a comical hand gesture.*) May I speak to you for a moment, sir?

PAOLINO: What do you want? I'm in the middle of a lesson and you know damned well that when I'm teaching . . .

ROSARIA: Of course I know. And that's why my interrupting you means that it's something important.

PAOLINO: (*To the students.*) Wait just a second. (*To Rosaria.*) Now what is it that is *so* important.

ROSARIA: A woman is here, with a little boy, and she says that she's a friend of yours.

PAOLINO: Is she the mother of one of my students?

ROSARIA: (*Suspiciously.*) I don't know. Could be. But she is very upset.

PAOLINO: Upset?

ROSARIA: Very. When she asked for you she turned red, white and a hundred other colors.

PAOLINO: But who is she? What's her name? I've told you a thousand times to ask the name of anyone who comes looking for me.

ROSARIA: I did. And she told me. Her name is—wait a minute—her name is Mrs. Per—Per, Per, Per . . .

PAOLINO: (*With a start, almost terrified, greatly agitated.*) Mrs. Perella?

ROSARIA: That's it.

PAOLINO: Oh my God. She's here. I wonder what's wrong. Good God. Wait a few minutes.

ROSARIA: So you do know her.

PAOLINO: (*Glares at her.*) Just tell her to wait.

ROSARIA: All right! All Right! (*She leaves.*)

PAOLINO: (*Trying to compose himself and control his agitation. He returns to his desk.*) Boys, we . . . we don't want to waste time, do we. Look, instead of history and geography, today I want you to do another translation.
GIGLIO & BELLI: No, sir, please.
PAOLINO: From Italian into Latin.
GIGLIO & BELLI: Please sir, not again.
GIGLIO: We did one yesterday.
BELLI: It's always Latin, Latin and more Latin.
PAOLINO: I can't help it if it's your weakest subject.
GIGLIO: We can't stand it anymore.
PAOLINO: That's ENOUGH!
BELLI: We don't even have our dictionaries.
PAOLINO: I'll find some for you. (*He hurries to the bookcase and gets two dictionaries.*) Here. One each.
GIGLIO: But sir . . .
PAOLINO: That's enough, I said.(*He takes a book from his desk and starts to leaf through it.*) Let's see. Translate . . . translate . . . (*As he's looking for a passage he becomes distracted and begins to talk to himself.*) Why did she come here? Why today? She's never done this before. (*He becomes aware that the two boys are straining to look at him and to see the book he holds in his hands, as if they were looking for the words he is mumbling. He recovers his composure.*) What are you looking at?
GIGLIO: Uh . . . the translation . . .
BELLI: What you were reading.
PAOLINO: Mind your own business. I want you to translate . . . yes, this passage here. It's quite brief. This will make me very happy. (*He goes to open the door of the small closet at the rear and motions to them with a hand gesture.*) Here, come here. I'm going to put you in this nice little room.
BELLI: (*Horrified.*) In there?
GIGLIO: (*Also horrified.*) Sir, how can we see in there?
PAOLINO: Just be patient. It's only for a few minutes. Let's go. (*He shoves them in.*) Each of you do your own work, I'm warning you. Now get busy. Don't waste time. (*He slams the door shut and runs to the other door to invite Mrs. Perella in.*) Mrs. Perella . . . come . . . please come in.

(*Mrs. Perella enters from the left with her son Nono. She is the embodiment of virtue, prudence and modesty. These qualities unfortunately can't negate the fact that she is two months pregnant—not yet noticeably so—by the private tutor of her son Nono, Paolino. She has come to confirm to her lover the suspicion that is now all too certain. Her modesty and Nono's presence will impede her from confirming it openly, but she conveys it with her eyes and even—without intending it—with the expression of her mouth which, in vain, is trying to suppress her extreme agitation. She holds a handkerchief to her lips and with the same compunction with which she would try to suppress tears, she is trying to hide abun-*

dant and symptomatic salivating. *She is extremely afflicted because her many virtues and exemplary modesty do not merit such a fate. Her eyes are downcast; she doesn't raise them so that her anguish and martyrdom, hidden from Nono, won't escape and reveal themselves to Paolino. She is dressed awkwardly, since fashion by its very nature makes virtuous people look awkward. She is forced to dress according to fashion and God only knows how she suffers. She speaks with a querulous voice, almost distant, as if she is really not speaking herself but is being manipulated by an invisible ventriloquist who is doing a bad imitation of a melancholy woman's voice. Occasionally she will forget and will have an outburst and speak in natural tones and modulation.*

Nono resembles a big, beautiful, friendly cat. He wears a magnificent big red tie with butterflies on it and a high rounded starched collar. It wouldn't be wrong if he wielded one of those sticks with a dog's head on it that boys carried. He often laughs and even more often he sniffles in order to spare the handkerchief which looks so nice in his jacket pocket, perfectly folded and unused.)

PAOLINO: (*At once exchanging a meaningful glance with Mrs. Perella and picking up from her look that she's warning him with her eyes to take heed of Nono's presence.*) Yes? . . .Oh, God . . . Yes? (*Turning to Nono, in response to her signal.*) Hello, Nono.

NONO: Good morning, sir.

PAOLINO: Good morning, dear Nono. You're a good boy, Nono, aren't you. Make yourself at home, Mrs. Perella. (*Sotto voce.*) Then there's no doubt. You're absolutely certain. (*Once again, but even more emphatically this time, she gives him an eye signal in Nono's direction.*) So, you've come to visit your teacher, my dear little Nono?

NONO: (*He shakes his finger "no" before he speaks—a habit with him.*) We're on our way to Santa Lucia, to the landing.

PAOLINO: Oh, really. To see the boats?

NONO: (*Again waving his finger.*) To find out when papa's ship gets in. (*Then, with a scheming smile, he looks to his mother who, just seated, is opening her mouth like a fish.*) But look how my mother opens her mouth again!

PAOLINO: (*In an outburst.*) Who? What do you mean, her mouth? (*Frightened by the sight of her open mouth.*) Oh, my God, what's the matter? What is it? (*He runs over to her while she, holding a handkerchief to her mouth, has retreated to the back of the stage, near the closet door.*)

MRS. PERELLA: (*Exhausted, she supports herself against one of the bookcases. While she's holding the handkerchief to her mouth she makes desperate signs to Paolino not to come any closer and to do something about Nono, for the love of God.*) For pity's sake. Please.

NONO: (*Smiling and calm, to Paolino, who is on the verge of collapse.*) She's been opening her mouth like that for three days now.

PAOLINO: Oh, it's nothing, Nono dear. Nothing. Your mother . . . your mother is just . . . yawning. That's it. She's yawning.

NONO: (*Makes his customary sign with his finger and then, with the same finger, points to her stomach.*) And what about there?
PAOLINO: (*With a scream.*) No! Blessed child, what are you saying?
NONO: It's a stomachache. She said so herself.
PAOLINO: (*Catching his breath.*) Of course . . . that's it. That's all it is, Nono, a little stomachache.
MRS. PERELLA: (*Groaning, still at the rear of the stage.*) Oh, for the love of God.
NONO: And look how she keeps spitting into her handkerchief.
MRS. PERELLA: Oh . . .
PAOLINO: Now really, Nono. Have you lost your mind? Such things to say about your mother!
NONO: But why not?
MRS. PERELLA: (*Grievously, with real force behind her words.*) He's been saying these things . . . even in front of the maid.
NONO: What's wrong with that?
PAOLINO: Nothing's wrong, but it's not polite to speak that way in front of a serving person.
MRS. PERELLA: What about his father? He'll tell his father as soon as he walks through the door. (*To Paolino, in a soft voice that nonetheless expresses her terror.*) His ship arrives today. Today!
NONO: (*Rejoicing, clapping his hands.*) Yes, today! Please send me on board with the sailor.
PAOLINO: Nono! Don't bother your mother.
NONO: (*Reassuring him.*) Oh, she's okay. They're gone now. (*To his mother.*) Please let me go on board, mother, please. I like it so much when papa directs the ship from the bridge, all dressed up in his big shiny coat and his captain's hat. Please say that I can go, mama, please.
MRS. PERELLA: I'll let you go, all right . . . (*To Paolino, indicating Nono.*) He'll be the death of me . . .
PAOLINO: Nono. I'm ashamed of you. Can't you see how upset your mother is?
NONO: It's funny when she opens her mouth this way . . . (*he imitates her*) like a fish . . .
PAOLINO: That's just great. Your mother suffers and you laugh. Wonderful. And you're going to tell your father that your mother opens her mouth like a fish so that he can laugh at her too, right. (*He goes to his desk and picks up a big picture book.*) Look, I was going to give this to you today.
NONO: *The Life of the Insects.* It's really nice. Is it for me?
PAOLINO: No. You're a bad boy and I'm not going to give it to you. (*At this point a loud knocking is heard from the little closet at the rear. At the same time we hear:*)
VOICES OF GIGLIO & BELLI: Sir, sir.
MRS. PERELLA: (*Standing by the door, she jumps, startled, and runs to the front of the*

stage, terrified.) Oh, my God, what's that.
PAOLINO: Nothing—just some animals. Two of my students—don't worry.
NONO: Good. Are they hiding in there?
PAOLINO: (*Goes to the door, opens it slightly, sticks his head in.*) What the hell do you want?
NONO: (*Trying to look through Paolino's legs.*) Is he punishing them in there?
MRS. PERELLA: Nono, come here.
GIGLIO'S VOICE: Can we have some light in here, even a candle, sir. We can't see.
BELLI'S VOICE: We can't even read the words in the dictionary.
PAOLINO: All right. Shut up and I'll bring you a candle! (*Slams the door.*)
NONO: Why are you hiding them in there?
PAOLINO: I'm not hiding them. They're working on a translation.
NONO: (*Frightened.*) In the dark?
PAOLINO: Of course not. I'm getting them some light.
NONO: In the meantime I'll just look at my book.
PAOLINO: No, I've decided not to give it to you now. (*Paolino goes out and returns at once with a lighted candle. While he's gone first Giglio and then Belli sticks his head out the door to look at Mrs. Perella, who is frightened and mortified. They look at her with malicious smiles and when they see Nono they stick out their tongues at him.*)
NONO: (*To Paolino, as he returns.*) They stuck their heads out the door!
MRS. PERELLA: (*Trembling.*) They saw me. They saw me!
NONO: First one of them did it, then the other. Then they went like this! (*Sticks out his tongue.*)
PAOLINO: I forgot to lock the door. Calm down. (*He goes to the door and shoves in the candle.*) Here's your candle. Now get down to work. (*He locks the door but now must attend to Nono.*) Now, do you really want this book?
NONO: Yes. You bought it for me, didn't you?
PAOLINO: Yes—and I'll give it to you if you promise . . .
NONO: Yes, yes . . . (*He sees his mother with her mouth open again.*) Look, see. It's no use. I don't say a word and she does it again.
PAOLINO: Good God, this is terrible. (*To Nono.*) Now, remember, you promised not to make fun of your mother anymore. (*He puts the book on a chair facing Mrs. Perella and Nono on another with its back toward her.*) Now be a good boy and look at the book by yourself. (*He approaches Mrs. Perella who is still struggling with the handkerchief at her mouth.*) This is dreadful. All of this screams out as proof . . .
MRS. PERELLA: I'm lost. Finished . . . There's no way out—only death.
PAOLINO: What are you saying?
MRS. PERELLA: There's no other choice.
PAOLINO: If you insist on talking this way you'll only make things worse.
MRS. PERELLA: But don't you understand. If this happens in front of *him*—
PAOLINO: Just make sure that it doesn't.

MRS. PERELLA: (*With an outburst in her normal voice.*) It's just like when I was expecting Nono.
PAOLINO: It's happened before? And he's aware of it?
MRS. PERELLA: Yes, and he would always laugh whenever he saw me that way, just like Nono is laughing now . . .
PAOLINO: Then if he sees—
MRS. PERELLA: I'm lost. It's all over.
PAOLINO: Can't you force yourself not to do it.
MRS. PERELLA: It just happens, I tell you. Suddenly. (*In her normal voice.*) It's an involuntary reaction.
NONO: (*Running, with the book in his hand.*) Look, mama, how pretty. A spider weaving his web.
PAOLINO: (*At first with an angry outburst, then recovering and reverting to a comically exaggerated affection.*) Leave her alone . . . my dear, sweet little Nono. Yes, it is a spider weaving his web. There are lots of other pretty creatures in there too, you know. Lots. So now show them to your mama later on . . . Little spiders, ants, butterflies . . . (*He leads Nono back to where he was.*) Now that's a good boy. (*Once again there is knocking at the rear closet door with the simultaneous cries.*)
VOICES OF GIGLIO & BELLI: Sir, sir.
PAOLINO: I'll kill them both. I swear to God I will. (*He runs to the back door and opens it.*) What do you want now? Can't you two stay still for fifteen minutes and do a translation that a fifth grader could do?
BELLI: (*Sticking his head out the door.*) Not only, but also, sir.
PAOLINO: What are you talking about, but also?
BELLI: It says that here: not only, but also. It's the adversative form, isn't it?
PAOLINO: Adversative? There's no such thing, you clown? Can't you see that it expresses a coordinative.
GIGLIO: (*Coming forward.*) That's what I told him. Increasing intensity of value.
PAOLINO: Even he knows that much. (*Indicates Nono.*) Not only, but also. Nono, how would you translate not only.
NONO: (*Jumping to his feet and standing at attention.*) *Non solum!*
PAOLINO: Very good. Is there any other way of expressing it?
NONO: *Non tantum.*
PAOLINO: Excellent. Any others?
GIGLIO: *Non modo,* sir, *non modo* or *tantummodo.*
PAOLINO: (*Pushing them back into the closet.*) So you do know it after all. The devil take you, both of you. (*He closes the door.*)
MRS. PERELLA: Oh God, the shame.
PAOLINO: Don't worry. You're the mother of one of my students. That's why I questioned Nono. Rosaria is the one we have to worry about.
MRS. PERELLA: The look she gave me!

PAOLINO: You were wrong to come here. I would have come to your house before evening.
MRS. PERELLA: But the ship docks at five. I had to warn you that there's no longer any doubt. Don't you see. It's definite now. What am I going to do?
PAOLINO: How long will he be here?
MRS. PERELLA: He's due to sail again tomorrow.
PAOLINO: Tomorrow!
MRS. PERELLA: For the Middle East. He'll be gone for another two months, at least.
PAOLINO: Then he'll only be here tonight.
MRS. PERELLA: But it will be like all the other times, you can be sure of that.
PAOLINO: No, it can't be.
MRS. PERELLA: What are you talking about?
PAOLINO: IT JUST CAN'T.
MRS. PERELLA: And why not? You don't seem to understand. I'm lost, Paolino, I'm lost. (*A knock is heard.*)
PAOLINO: Who is it?
ROSARIA: (*Opening the door.*) Pardon me but I have to get the key that Toto left for his brother the doctor. It's here on the table.
PAOLINO: (*Struck by an idea.*) The doctor? Wait! Is the doctor here now?
ROSARIA: He came for his key.
PAOLINO: (*Takes the key from her hand.*) Give it to me. Tell him to wait a few minutes. I've got to talk to him.
ROSARIA: The poor man's exhausted. He's been up all night.
PAOLINO: Tell him to wait. That's an order!
ROSARIA: Yes sir, whatever you say. (*She leaves.*)
MRS. PERELLA: (*Frightened.*) Oh, God, Paolino, what are you going to do? Why do you want to see the doctor?
PAOLINO: I don't know yet. I'll just talk to him. Ask for his help. His advice.
MRS. PERELLA: What kind of help. For me?
PAOLINO: Yes. Let me take care of it. Let me try . . .
MRS. PERELLA: Paolino, NO. What are you talking about, for God's sake?
PAOLINO: But I *have* to help you.
MRS. PERELLA: You'll only make things worse by compromising me.
PAOLINO: Do you want to die?
MRS. PERELLA: I would rather die than suffer this shame.
PAOLINO: Don't be crazy. I'm here to help you. Leave it to me.
MRS. PERELLA: What are you going to do?
PAOLINO: I told you, I don't know yet. But I'll find something. The doctor is an old friend. We're like brothers. Let me talk to him. You go home now and I'll see you at your house before the ship gets in. I'll come for dinner. (*He goes over to Nono, who is still reading his book.*) Now, Nono, you take the book and go home with mama. Later on I'll come visit you and write a nice

inscription: To my good friend Nono in recognition of his progress in Latin. All right?

NONO: Oh, yes. It's a beautiful book. The words too.

PAOLINO: Give me a kiss.

MRS. PERELLA: And thank your teacher, Nono.

NONO: (*Making his customary gesture with his finger.*) There's no need to.

MRS. PERELLA: What do you mean, no need to?

NONO: I've already thanked him. Didn't I?

PAOLINO: Yes, you did. He did. Now it's time to go, Nono.

NONO: You're coming to our house for dinner?

PAOLINO: Yes. And I'll even bring some of that pastry you like so much.

NONO: Good. See you later. You're coming soon?

PAOLINO: In a little while. (*Softly.*) Mrs. Perella, be brave.

MRS. PERELLA: Good-bye. (*They exit through the kitchen door with Paolino. The stage is empty for a moment.*)

PAOLINO: (*Ushering the doctor in.*) Come in, please. Have a seat. (*Points to an easy chair.*)

DR. PULEIO: (*A handsome man, around thirty, blond, with glasses.*) No, really, I'd love to but I've got to go home and get some sleep, my dear friend.

PAOLINO: Well you'll just have to change your schedule today.

DR. PULEIO: What?

PAOLINO: I have to talk to you about a very serious matter.

DR. PULEIO: And it's more important than my sleep. You're out of your mind.

PAOLINO: Are you a doctor or aren't you?

DR. PULEIO: Oh, you need some professional advice?

PAOLINO: Yes. Right away.

DR. PULEIO: That's a different matter then. Start talking.

PAOLINO: I *have* been talking. I told you it was urgent and now you want me to talk to you after you've told me that you want to go home to bed.

DR. PULEIO: Look, I'm exhausted. I'm sorry, but there's nothing to discuss. I need some rest after a night on call and I should have the right to go home to bed.

PAOLINO: I'll get you some coffee.

DR. PULEIO: I'd rather you just told me what's on your mind.

PAOLINO: I know what I'll do. I'll climb up on that bookcase and jump off. Then you'll have to stay here for a few hours to take care of my broken leg.

DR. PULEIO: Brilliant! That would make me fix your broken leg but it wouldn't make me talk to you.

PAOLINO: But I'll talk to you while you're setting my leg.

DR. PULEIO: You can talk all you want. I won't be paying any attention because I'll be taking care of your leg.

PAOLINO: But at least you won't be home sleeping!

DR. PULEIO: What good will that do you? I'll lose my sleep, you'll break your leg and we'll both be wasting our time. On the other hand, if you let me go home and rest for a couple of hours . . .

PAOLINO: I can't. There's no time for that. You have to help me right away.

DR. PULEIO: What kind of help? What are you talking about?

PAOLINO: My life, Nino. My life. And if you don't help me I'm finished— a dead man— you can just bury me in the ground. And it's not just me. We're talking about four lives, no five now, almost five. At this point I could be responsible for a massacre.

DR. PULEIO: What? Nothing less than that?

PAOLINO: It's no joke, I swear to you. It could be a bloody slaughter.

DR. PULEIO: Will you calm down and tell me what's going on? What happened?

PAOLINO: You've got to come up with a cure right now, this morning.

DR. PULEIO: What kind of cure?

PAOLINO: I don't know. Let me tell you.

DR. PULEIO: If this depends on me . . .

PAOLINO: Yes, it may be the kind of cure only you can prescribe.

DR. PULEIO: All right! Let's hear about it. (*He sits.*)

PAOLINO: Now listen carefully.

DR. PULEIO: Of course, for God's sake. Now tell me about it.

PAOLINO: I'm warning you. I'm talking to you like a brother now. No, the hell with that. A doctor is like a priest hearing confession, right?

DR. PULEIO: Certainly. We have our professional secrecy too.

PAOLINO: Perfect. Then I'll talk to you under the seal of the confessional. Like a brother *and* a priest. (*Pause.*) Nino. (*He covers his eyes, extends a hand and joins the index finger and the thumb, as if he's weighing the words he's about to utter.*) Perella has two homes.

DR. PULEIO: Perella. And who is Perella?

PAOLINO: (*Erupting.*) Perella! The sea captain, for God's sake. (*Lowers his voice, remembering Giglio and Belli in the closet.*) Captain Perella. General Navigation. Long distance sailor. Commander of the Segesta.

DR. PULEIO: Fine. I get the picture. Captain Perella. I don't know him.

PAOLINO: Oh, you don't? So much the better. He's got two homes. One here and one in Naples.

DR. PULEIO: He's a lucky guy. Two homes. So?

PAOLINO: (*Looks at him squarely, summoning all the rage he can.*) It seems like nothing to you? A married man, with a son, who's vile enough to take advantage of his position as a captain and has another home, in another place, with another woman. You see nothing wrong with that? It's absolutely monstrous, for God's sake.

DR. PULEIO: No one would disagree with you? But what does this have to do with *you*? Where do *you* come in?

PAOLINO: What does this have to do with me, you ask?

DR. PULEIO: Is she a relative of yours, this Mrs. Perella? (*Again there is knocking from the closet door and . . .*)
VOICES OF GIGLIO & BELLI: Sir, sir.
PAOLINO: Not again. Today has been one disaster after another. (*Without getting up, shouting toward the back.*) What do you want now?
BELLI'S VOICE: We've finished, sir.
GIGLIO'S VOICE: Open the door. We are suffocating in here. Let us out.
PAOLINO: Hold on. You can't possibly have finished.
GIGLIO'S VOICE: But we're all done, sir.
BELLI'S VOICE: We can't breathe. Open the door!
PAOLINO: I'll do no such thing. Read over your work and be quiet. The hour isn't over yet. (*To the doctor.*) It shouldn't concern me, right, because we're not related. And if we were?
DR. PULEIO: Well, if she were a relative . . .
PAOLINO: But she's not. She's just a poor woman who is suffering the agonies of hell. An honest woman who's been betrayed in a beastly way, don't you see? By her husband. Do I have to be her relative in order to be outraged, disgusted, incensed?
DR. PULEIO: And where do I fit into all of this?
PAOLINO: Will you please let me finish. It's easy for you to remain calm, while I'm dying. Can't you see that I'm dying? Give me your hand. (*He extends his hand to shake the doctor's and then squeezes it as hard as he can until the doctor wants to scream.*)
DR. PULEIO: Oww! That hurts! Have you gone out of your mind?
PAOLINO: That's so you'll feel what it's like when someone else's pain is at stake. You look outside yourself, at other people, and they don't really concern you. What do they matter to you? Nothing. Images that float by. That's all. Well, you've got to *feel* what's inside them. Immerse yourself in their pain—really feel it—like that . . . (*indicates the hand the doctor is still massaging*) what I just made you feel.
DR. PULEIO: Thank you very much, my dear friend. But I have enough problems of my own. Everyone does. Don't you realize how ridiculous you are right now? (*He laughs.*)
PAOLINO: A real barrel of laughs, isn't it? I know, the clear, open sight of bare emotions can be very exhilarating. But they're also the saddest, the most agonizing things . . . Passions can make everybody laugh. No doubt about it. But have you ever really felt true passion—or are you so used to covering it over with a protective shield of lies that you can't even sympathize with a poor guy like me whose misfortune can no longer be controlled or hidden. For God's sake, Nino, feel for me. Inside yourself, feel for me. I'm truly suffering.
DR PULEIO: But what are you suffering from? You didn't say that you were in pain. You were going on about this Mrs. Perella.

PAOLINO: Exactly.

DR. PULEIO: Mrs. Perella is making you suffer?

PAOLINO: Yes, Nino. But you don't understand. Let me explain it to you. This Captain Perella, this wonderful Captain Perella, he's not satisfied to cheat on his wife, to have another home in Naples, as I told you, with another woman. No—he has three or four children there, by her, and one here, by his wife. *And he doesn't want to have any more.*

DR. PULEIO: Well, five kids . . . that sounds like enough to me.

PAOLINO: You think so, do you? With his wife he has one, just one. The others are illegitimate. If he has any more by the one in Naples he can get rid of them, in a foundling home, if he wants to. But with his wife it's a different story. He can't get rid of a legitimate child, can he?

DR. PULEIO: Of course not.

PAOLINO: So what does all this mean? I'll tell you. For the last three years, whenever the dirty two-timer is in port here, he has found the least excuse to pick a fight with his wife and then go sleep by himself. He slams the bedroom door in her face and then she has to spend the night on the couch. The next day he goes back to sea and that's that. It's been like this for three years now.

DR. PULEIO: (*With commiseration, but still unable to suppress a smile.*) The poor lady . . . slamming the door in her face like that.

PAOLINO: In her face . . . and the couch . . . and the next day . . . (*Uses a hand gesture to indicate that he takes off.*)

DR. PULEIO: The poor thing. But look.

PAOLINO: Is that all you can say?

DR. PULEIO: What more can I say? Look, if you don't mind my saying so, I still don't see where I come in. What can I do? My heart goes out to her . . . It's a real shame.

PAOLINO: And that's that. What if she were your sister, if Perella were your brother-in-law and you knew that he was betraying his wife that way . . .

DR. PULEIO: I'd wring his neck.

PAOLINO: There, you see! You'd wring his neck!

DR. PULEIO: Of course I would. Any good brother would do the same thing.

PAOLINO: Well, what about if this poor woman doesn't have any brothers— or anyone else who can take this Captain Perella by the neck and make him live up to his marriage vows. Are we just supposed to let her suffer, a woman like that, without giving her any help? Does that seem fair? Does that seem right?

DR. PULEIO: Yes, but . . . you . . .

PAOLINO: What about me?

DR. PULEIO: Excuse me for asking, but first of all, how do you come to know about all of this?

PAOLINO: How do I know. . . ? I know . . . I know . . . because . . . well, for

... for a year now I've ... I've been giving Latin lessons to the boy, Perella's eleven-year-old son.

DR. PULEIO: So that was the woman who left here a few minutes ago, with the boy carrying the book.

PAOLINO: (*Almost in a fit.*) Remember your professional secrecy!!

DR. PULEIO: You can rest assured ...

PAOLINO: That woman is virtue incarnate. You can't know, Nino, you can't possibly know how much she's moved me, with all the tears that woman has shed. The goodness, the refined feelings, the purity. And on top of it she's so beautiful. Well, you saw her.

DR. PULEIO: Actually, I didn't. She'd lowered her veil over her face.

PAOLINO: Well, take my word for it, she's beautiful. If she were ugly then I might understand. But she's not. Just the opposite. And she's still young. To see her treated this way—betrayed, scorned, cast aside like an old dishrag. You can see how she would have resisted. Who wouldn't have rebelled? Who could blame her? (*Almost thrusting his hands in the doctor's face.*) Can you dare condemn her?

DR. PULEIO: Me? No. Certainly not!

PAOLINO: If you could only see what you're condemning.

DR. PULEIO: But I'm not. If it's true that her husband treats her this way ...

PAOLINO: He does! You don't have any doubts about what I've been saying?

DR. PULEIO: Of course not.

PAOLINO: Then, my dear friend, help me save her. Because this poor woman finds herself on the edge of a precipice. Help me, help me before she goes over the edge. We have to save her!

DR. PULEIO: How?

PAOLINO: How? Just think for a moment. What could be the worst disaster for a woman left like this, for three years, by her husband? She finds herself ...

DR. PULEIO: (*Hesitantly, not wanting to understand.*) What?

PAOLINO: (*Hesitantly, but in a way as to leave no doubt.*) Yes ...in a terrible situation. Desperate.

DR. PULEIO: Now Paolino, wait a minute. I don't perform ... Look, I could go to jail for ...

PAOLINO: You imbecile. What are you talking about? What do you think I'm asking you to do anyway?

DR. PULEIO: Well, I assumed ... since I'm a doctor—and you're telling me that she's ...

PAOLINO: You idiot! So that's why you thought I wanted you? I'm talking about an honest woman. Didn't I say that she was virtue incarnate?

DR. PULEIO: Forget I even suggested it.

PAOLINO: That's easy for you to say.

DR. PULEIO: Look here. If you're not asking me to ...

PAOLINO: What do you think . . . that I would ask you to break the law—and do something that's wrong not only for her but for me as well? Do you think I'm such a scoundrel to be capable of something like that? What I'm asking you for is . . . Oh, I was crazy even to consider it.
DR. PULEIO: (*Losing all patience.*) Will you just tell me what you want from me. I-do-not-understand.
PAOLINO: I want what is right. I want what is honest. I want what is moral.
DR. PULEIO: Which is?
PAOLINO: (*Shouting.*) That Perella be a good husband. That's what I want. That tonight he won't slam the door in his wife's face. This is what I want.
DR. PULEIO: You want me to . . . (*He breaks out into uncontrollable laughter.*) I . . . I thought you wanted . . . ha, ha, ha . . . And what you really wanted . . . ha, ha, ha . . . you want to lead the horse to water and make him drink. Ha, ha, ha!
PAOLINO: (*Looks at the doctor, who continues to laugh, squarely in the face.*) What's so damn funny, you brute? We're talking about a real-life tragedy and you're laughing your head off. A woman's honor, her very life is at stake and you sit here laughing. Not to mention me. (*Resolutely gesturing to the doctor.*) You know what will happen? After three months at sea Perella will return home this evening. He'll spend only one night here. Just one night. Tonight. Then tomorrow he sails for the Middle East and he'll be gone for another two months. Do you get the picture now? If we don't take advantage of this one night then everything is lost.
DR. PULEIO: (*Struggling to control himself.*) All right, fine, but, but I . . .
PAOLINO: Stop laughing, damn it. Stop laughing or I'll throttle you.
DR. PULEIO: I'm not laughing.
PAOLINO: Go ahead. Mock my desperation if you want—but for God's sake, help me. There's got to be a solution—you're a doctor—You must have a way.
DR. PULEIO: To make sure that the captain will sleep with his wife tonight?
PAOLINO: Exactly.
DR. PULEIO: In the service of virtue, of course.
PAOLINO: To save both this poor martyr of a woman and myself. Are you still laughing?
DR. PULEIO: No! Can't you see that I'm sympathetic. But this captain. How old is he?
PAOLINO: I don't know exactly. Around forty I'd guess.
DR. PULEIO: In good health.
PAOLINO: He's a real beast.
DR. PULEIO: And you said that he's just returning from three months at sea.
PAOLINO: Right. But remember, he's already stopped at Naples.
DR. PULEIO: Ah . . . where his other home is.
PAOLINO: Precisely—the bastard—he always does it this way.

DR. PULEIO: He stops at Naples first?
PAOLINO: Yes!
DR. PULEIO: Then tonight he has to realize that he has a home here too.
PAOLINO: And a wife.
DR. PULEIO: Who's waiting for him.
PAOLINO: (*Sensing a touch of irony in the doctor's tone and irritated by it.*) Maybe you think we should try reasoning with him?
DR. PULEIO: No, no. As God is my witness, he's in the wrong. But perhaps, that is, possibly there's more to it . . .
PAOLINO: Not at all. There's only his wrongdoing and the consequences of that wrongdoing.
DR. PULEIO: Exactly . . . yes . . . a consequence that perhaps you should have . . .
PAOLINO: (*Suddenly interrupting.*) But who should have . . . not me, not her. That's for damn sure. Now listen to me. Who's at fault here? The intention is what counts, right. Not the results. If you mean well, then you can't be blamed for whatever happens. I rest my case. It's just rotten luck, that's all. Look, it's like if you own a piece of land and you abandon it. Now there's a tree on this land and you don't take care of the tree—just like it doesn't belong to anyone. All right, somebody comes along and picks some fruit from the tree, eats it and throws away the seeds. Actually *you've* thrown away the seeds by the very fact that the abandoned fruit grew on your tree. So, some time later another tree sprouts up, from one of the seeds. Did you want that tree? Of course not. But neither did the poor seed want to sprout up on that land. Now then, who does this new tree belong to? It's *yours*, naturally, because *you* own the land.
DR. PULEIO: Mine? No thank you.
PAOLINO: (*Almost attacking him, furiously grabbing his arm and shaking him.*) Then take care of your land, for God's sake. Take care of it. Make sure that somebody doesn't come along and pick the fruit off your abandoned tree!
DR. PULEIO: All right, all right. I'm not arguing. But I don't really enter into this. It's the captain who will do it.
PAOLINO: And he has to do it. He just has to. And you say he will?
DR. PULEIO: By God, we'll just make sure he does . . .
PAOLINO: (*Kissing him with a vehement effusion of gratitude and admiration.*) Nino, you're a god! But tell me, how? HOW?
DR. PULEIO: Wait a minute. (*Pauses—starts to think.*) Does the captain eat at home?
PAOLINO: Yes, around six, right after his ship docks. In fact, I'm invited to join them tonight.
DR. PULEIO: Fine . . . Now, you wouldn't go there empty-handed, would you?
PAOLINO: No . . . as a matter of fact, I promised the boy that I'd bring some

pastry.

DR. PULEIO: Perfect. (*Cutting short.*) Now listen. You go to the bakery and buy this pastry.

PAOLINO: (*Still not comprehending.*) What? And where are you going?

DR. PULEIO: To my brother's drugstore.

PAOLINO: What are you going to do there?

DR. PULEIO: Just wait for me there. At least give me the chance to go home and wash my face. I won't be able to go to bed now.

PAOLINO: Oh, no you don't. I'm not leaving you, Nino. Not unless you tell me . . .

DR. PULEIO: What more can I tell you. Go to the bakery and buy the pastry and give me the key to my house.

PAOLINO: But the pastry is for the boy.

DR. PULEIO: Fine. But you can also offer some to the lady, I should think, *and to the captain.* (*Looks at him meaningfully.*) Do I make myself clear?

PAOLINO: The pastry?

DR. PULEIO: Exactly. Now get going. Leave the rest to me. Where is my key.

PAOLINO: No. You can't have it. You'll just go to bed.

DR. PULEIO: Don't worry. I'm passed the point of sleeping now.

PAOLINO: You can wash your face here.

DR. PULEIO: Let's get going. We're wasting time. You're like a little kid. Now come on, give me the key . . .

PAOLINO: (*Dangling key in front of him.*) Here. I'm trusting you. Take care, Nino, my life goes with this. (*He has another attack of doubt.*) What are you going to do with this pastry?

DR. PULEIO: I told you to leave it to me.

PAOLINO: Can you really . . . with the help of science? (*Reviving, with a scream of disdain.*) Oh, God . . . to come to this!

DR. PULEIO: Now what?

PAOLINO: You think that all there is to know about me is centered in this one idiotic problem for which I had to ask your help. For *me* to have to ask help, for this, to science . . . and to come to you, the representative of science who uses science to improve our lives, while I love science disinterestedly. I venerate knowledge at the cost of so many sacrifices.

DR. PULEIO: Look here. If you're going to . . .

PAOLINO: No listen. It's just to come to . . . (*Snorts.*) Ufft. My stomach is churning inside of me. To come to this . . . without knowing why . . . for nothing . . . for a little pity I offered to a woman whom I saw crying and who at first didn't even want to tell me why—who had to be forced into talking about it. Then to be faced—today, tomorrow and then . . . to find myself in a trap like this—and all because of the bestial cruelty of a bastard like that—to be in a situation like this—it's ludicrous. Doesn't it seem that way to you? You laughed at me—you laughed.

DR. PULEIO: No, Paolino.
PAOLINO: Yes, I made you laugh . . . because I want . . .
DR. PULEIO: To make sure that the captain does his duty as a husband . . .
PAOLINO: Because I can't do anything else—understand!
DR. PULEIO: It's the right thing to do. Morality . . .
PAOLINO: But it's your morality, not mine. I'd like to kill him—and I swear I will kill him, if he doesn't do his duty, this big shot captain. I'm an honest man—I'd marry her myself, right this second, to make things right.
DR. PULEIO: Of course, you would. But let's get going. Let's not talk about it anymore. We've got work to do.
PAOLINO: Let's go—I'll kill him, I swear.
DR. PULEIO: Let's hope that won't be necessary.
PAOLINO: Will twenty be enough?
DR. PULEIO: Twenty what?
PAOLINO: Twenty pieces of pastry.
DR. PULEIO: That's too much.
PAOLINO: Listen, I'll get thirty . . . forty. (*He's about to leave with the doctor when there's very loud pounding from the back and very loud screams.*)
VOICES OF GIGLIO & BELLI: Professor. Sir, sir. Open the door, for God's sake. Are you going to leave us in here all day?
PAOLINO: (*To the doctor.*) Wait . . . my students. I'd forgotten they were still here. (*Runs and opens the door.*)
GIGLIO & BELLI: (*They come out dishevelled, gasping for air, furious, throwing their books and dictionaries on the floor and protesting in unison.*) This is high-handed injustice. Tyranny! We were almost suffocated in there. We're not coming back here again.
PAOLINO: (*Running to placate them.*) Now boys, calm down, calm down.

END OF ACT I

ACT II

The dining room of the Perella home. There is a veranda at the rear with a wide vista of the sea. There are two side exits to the left—the closest to the proscenium is to the kitchen, the other to the captain's bedroom. Between the two doors is a flower stand with five flowerpots well in view. On the right side there is another entrance, along with glass cases containing an earthenware dinner service, a credenza, then a sofa with a mirror in back of it. There is also an easy chair and a little table. The dining room table is carefully set, for four people. On the walls are hung four seascapes, old photographs and here and there esoteric objects that are souvenirs from Captain Perella's voyages.

The afternoon of the same day as Act I. It will gradually become evening until, by the close of the Act, moonlight will be streaming in from the veranda. Paolino is seated at the little table with Nono, looking at the pages of a notebook of Latin translations and putting marks under each translation with a red and blue pencil.

PAOLINO: And here we can put a nice nine.
NONO: Another nine! (*Claps his hands exultantly.*) Good! So far, then, I have three eights, two nines and a ten.
PAOLINO: That's right. And as soon as your father gets home you can show him your notebook.
NONO: Sure. (*Begins to count on his fingers.*)
PAOLINO: Because—pay attention—today you have to do everything possible to make your father happy.
NONO: (*Not paying attention, continuing to count.*) All right . . .

PAOLINO: *(Following up his point.)* And stop fidgeting. What are you counting?
NONO: Wait a minute . . . three. *(With his right hand he holds three fingers of his left hand.)* Then four and five. *(Shows the five fingers of his left hand.)* Six and seven. *(Shows the index finger and thumb of his right hand.)* Eight, nine and ten. *(Shows, one by one, the other three fingers of the right hand.)* That makes half a lira!
PAOLINO: What do you mean, half a lira?
NONO: Yes, half a lira. That's swell. You see, papa gives me a penny for every eight—and since you gave me three eights, that makes three cents. Then two pennies for each nine—and there are two of them, so that's four cents. And the ten is worth three. So . . . three and four are seven and three more makes ten—which adds up to half a lira.
PAOLINO: Very good. Does that make you happy?
NONO: Me. Of course it does. But he won't be terribly pleased.
PAOLINO: What are you talking about? Why won't he be happy?
NONO: He used to give me three cents for a nine and five for a ten. But then, seeing that you were giving away the eights, nines and tens . . .
PAOLINO: Is that right? He said that—that I was giving the grades away?
NONO: Yes, the last time he was home he grabbed the notebook and threw it into the air, like this *(Nono does it, with disdain)* and shouted, For God's sake, this teacher is giving away eights, nines and tens like they were . . .
PAOLINO: And he really got upset over it?
NONO: That's why the pay scale went down.
PAOLINO: *(At once.)* All right then . . . *(he snatches back the notebook from Nono and begins madly marking)* we'll take care of that right away . . . we'll make this a five, this a six and this one here a seven.
NONO: *(Screaming as if a dentist were pulling a tooth out.)* Don't! Stop it! What about my half a lira?
PAOLINO: I'll see to that, Nono. Here . . . here. *(Takes out his change purse from his pocket.)* I'll give it to you.
NONO: But I don't want it from you.
PAOLINO: But you must, my boy. I know how important it is for your father to be happy. If you tell me that this makes him angry instead . . . well . . . Here, take it—what difference does it make whether you get the money from me or your father?
NONO: *(Pounding his feet.)* No, no, I want the grades. I want my eights, nines and tens.
PAOLINO: But to tell the truth, you really don't deserve them. You haven't truly earned them.
NONO: Then why did you give them to me?
PAOLINO: Because . . . well, because I didn't know they were costing your father money and were upsetting him. We don't want to do *anything* to upset your father, Nono. And today, today of all days, we must be especially cheerful. So you take this half lira as a secret reward from your

teacher—and just make sure you don't breathe a word about it to your father. I'm giving it to you not because you deserve nines and tens, but as a reward for the progress you've made.
NONO: Like you wrote in the book you gave me?
PAOLINO: Exactly. Just like I wrote in the book.
GRAZIA: (*Entering from the kitchen. She's an old woman with a sullen, equine face.*) Mrs. Perella?
PAOLINO: (*Pointing to the door at right.*) I think she's in there, Grazia.
GRAZIA: (*Indicating Nono.*) Then he can go and tell her that the sailor just got here.
NONO: (*Breaking into a shout.*) The sailor! That means papa's arrived. I'm going on board! I'm going on board! (*Starts to run into the kitchen.*)
PAOLINO: Wait a minute, Nono. Where are you going? Come here. First you have to tell your mother.
NONO: She knows, she knows. (*About to run off.*)
PAOLINO: Stay here I said. (*To Grazia.*) Will you please go and tell her.
NONO: But what if she already knows?
GRAZIA: (*Going to knock at the door, mumbling to herself.*) What a madhouse! (*She knocks at the door and without waiting for a response she enters.*)
NONO: (*Who has stopped near the kitchen, yells into it.*) Sailor! Sailor! Come in here!
SAILOR: (*Entering at once.*) Here I am! (*He bends down and opens his arms to receive Nono on his chest. Nono has leaped at him and put his arms around his neck.*) Ah. Long live the admiral
NONO: Take me to papa. Right now! (*Mrs. Perella enters from the right, dressed with such precise and extraordinary care as to make her appear even more awkward.*)
SAILOR: (*To Nono, who is still in his arms.*) Let's see what your mother has to say. (*Tips his cap to her.*) At your service, ma'am.
MRS. PERELLA: Has the ship already docked?
SAILOR: It was just about to, ma'am. It should be in by now.
NONO: Let's go! I want to watch them.
SAILOR: Don't worry. It will take a while. First they have to lower the gangplank.
MRS. PERELLA: Be careful, Nono. I'm putting him in your care, Filippo.
SAILOR: Don't worry, ma'am. You can trust old Filippo. See you later. Let's go see what your papa is up to. (*To Nono, who is still in his arms. They exit through the kitchen.*)

(*As soon as Nono and the sailor have left, Paolino turns to Mrs. Perella, who is the essence of modesty as effected through the clumsy encumberance of her extraordinary garb.*)

PAOLINO: Oh, no, no, no, no, my dear. What on earth have you done to yourself? Not like this!

MRS. PERELLA: I'm getting ready.
PAOLINO: But for what? You need a completely different approach.
MRS. PERELLA: Why?
PAOLINO: Because this is all wrong. It won't work.
MRS. PERELLA: You want me to do more than this? God only knows what it's cost me to do this much!
PAOLINO: I understand. But it's all wrong, my love. Everything may depend on the first impression. When he first sees you he has to find you enticing. The way you're dressed now, he won't. I know how difficult it was even to go this far. But it's not enough.
MRS. PERELLA: Oh God, then what now?
PAOLINO: The sacrifice you're being called on to make is enormous, my love, I know. For a woman like you, chaste and pure, to stoop to making yourself appetizing to a beast like that. But you *must* do it—and go all the way.
MRS. PERELLA: (*Hesitant, with her eyes lowered to the ground.*) Does that mean a lower neckline?
PAOLINO: Yes, much lower, much!
MRS. PERELLA: Oh my God, no.
PAOLINO: We don't have any choice. Your body has graces, an abundance of graces, which you jealously guard like a shrine. Now you have to expose them to a little violence.
MRS. PERELLA: Please Paolino, no. What are you saying? Don't you realize that it will be useless anyway. He never pays attention to me.
PAOLINO: Today we have to force him to pay attention. Since this animal doesn't appreciate the beauty of hidden graces, we'll put them right under his nose. Leave it to me. (*He approaches her, with his hands in front.*) Look, like this, please.
MRS. PERELLA: (*Upset, to the point of nausea, at what he has revealed, as she covers up her bosom.*) Oh. For God's sake, he's seen them before, Paolino.
PAOLINO: (*Pursuing her.*) You have to remind him.
MRS. PERELLA: It's no use. He won't pay any attention.
PAOLINO: But that's because, my love—and this is why I respect you, what makes me care for you and adore you so much—you've never known how to take advantage . . .
MRS. PERELLA: (*Almost horror-stricken.*) Take advantage? How?
PAOLINO: See, you can't even imagine how it's done. The others, though, they know all too well.
MRS. PERELLA: But what do they do?
PAOLINO: Nothing. That's the point. They don't cover themselves up like this. And then . . . Go away, you're driving me crazy. Don't think you're the only one who's paying for this. Think what it's costing me to get you ready so you can be with someone else. (*Raising his arm heavenward.*) God, why do I have to make this beauty appealing to such a beast? (*Back to Mrs.*

Perella.) But we have to. It's our only hope. And there's no time to lose. First of all, take that blouse off. You look like you're going to a funeral. Purple's a depressing color. We need something bright, something that really screams out—like red.

MRS. PERELLA: I don't have anything red.

PAOLINO: Then wear the Japanese silk blouse that shows you off so well.

MRS. PERELLA: But it's got a high neckline.

PAOLINO: Then for God's sake we'll just lower the neckline. We have to pull out all the stops. We'll fold the edges down inside, here, in front, and then we'll pin them with a lace border. But it's got to be open—almost down to here. (*Indicates far down on her bosom.*)

MRS. PERELLA: (*Shocked.*) No! Not that far!

PAOLINO: Yes. It's got to be that low. And you've got to do something with your hair too, for God's sake. Get rid of that little curl on your forehead. Try a big spring curl there, in the middle, and two more that come down your cheeks and then curl up.

MRS. PERELLA: (*Not understanding.*) But why spring curls, like that? I don't understand.

PAOLINO: Because I say so. Just do what I tell you. Don't make me lose time explaining. Curls on your cheeks like this—(*tracing them with his finger*) like an inverted question mark. One here, another here and a third there. (*Indicates the forehead, then one cheek and the other.*) If you won't do it yourself, then I will. Now, go and get ready. (*Pushes her to the door at right.*) And make sure that the neckline is low enough. While you're doing that, I'll make sure that the table is set for the meal we have to serve that beast. (*She exits right, leaving the door open. Paolino moves to the table and examines it carefully, adjusting, here and there, glasses and silverware.*)

PAOLINO: (*While he's fussing with the table.*) Let's see. This goes here. And this here. And that over there. Now why hasn't that imbecile Toto arrived yet. He said he would come in five minutes—well, Mr. Pharmacist, it's been an hour already.

MRS. PERELLA: (*Screaming from inside.*) Ah!

PAOLINO: What have you done?

MRS. PERELLA: (*From inside.*) I pricked myself with a pin.

PAOLINO: Is it bleeding?

MRS. PERELLA: (*From inside.*) No. I don't even have a drop left in my veins.

PAOLINO: I know, my love. And you need it so much, my pet, to give a little color to your cheeks.

MRS. PERELLA: (*From inside.*) It would just add to my shame.

PAOLINO: Don't worry. You're much too nervous to betray your shame by blushing. But I've thought of that too, don't worry. I have everything here that we'll need. (*Takes from his pocket a little box containing rouge and other makeup equipment and places it on the end table.*) That imbecile Toto hasn't arrived yet with the pastry. I'm on pins and needles. I should have known better than to trust him. If he doesn't get here in time. But he insisted—go on, I'll catch up with you in five minutes . . .

MRS. PERELLA: (*From the other room, crying.*) God . . . God . . . God . . .

PAOLINO: What's the matter now? Did you prick yourself again? Are you crying? (*Looks inside and stops—looks upward again.*) She having an attack—her mouth is open again!

MRS. PERELLA: (*From the other room, groaning.*) I'm so humiliated.

GRAZIA: (*Knocking at the door, then from outside.*) Excuse me.

PAOLINO: Come in.

GRAZIA: (*Entering, in a nasty tone of voice.*) There's a man here with a box and he asked for *you*.

PAOLINO: Oh, it's Toto, at last. Tell him to come in.

GRAZIA: Here?

PAOLINO: Yes, here . . . if you don't mind.

GRAZIA: Who am I to mind? If you want him to come in, I'll show him in—and that's that.

PAOLINO: Yes, please, in here . . . excuse me.

GRAZIA: What a madhouse! (*She leaves.*)

PAOLINO: We'll pull this thing off yet! (*Then as he rushes to close the door to Mrs. Perella's room, he announces.*) The pastry's here.

TOTO: (*From without.*) May I come in?

PAOLINO: Come on in, Toto. (*Toto enters, holding a box hidden behind his back.*) Five minutes, huh?

TOTO: Calm down. This is a delicate matter, Paolino. I'm only half responsible here. There's my brother too. And an innocent party is involved as well.

PAOLINO: (*Jumping at him.*) An innocent party! Who? Who's innocent? Do you dare say that someone is innocent. Him! Innocent? Look what he's forcing us to do—at the cost of making my heart burst with rage, anguish, desperation. Someone like me, who has never pretended before in my life, who has always shouted the truth in everyone's face. I'm forced to use a trick like this, with the help of an idiot like you.

TOTO: That's not what I meant at all. What could you be thinking of? I was referring to the little boy, Paolino. There is a little boy here, isn't there?

PAOLINO: Oh, you were talking about the boy.

TOTO: Of course I meant the boy. If I confused you by saying an innocent party, I'm sorry . . .

PAOLINO: No, I'm the one to apologize. Please forgive me, my friend. I'm in such a state. Have you brought what you were supposed to bring?

TOTO: That's what I've been trying to tell you. Since there's a child involved —you understand—I thought . . . God willing . . .

PAOLINO: Fine . . . all right . . .

TOTO: And I didn't want . . . I certainly didn't want . . .
PAOLINO: Just come to the point. What didn't you want? And what have you done instead?
TOTO: With the pastries? I ate them.
PAOLINO: You ate them? Forty pieces of pastry!
TOTO: Well, half of them. I'm saving the rest for my brother, tonight.
PAOLINO: What have you brought me, then?
TOTO: It won't make any difference, don't worry. In fact it will be even better. You'll see. (*Shows him.*) It's a beautiful cream cake, a St. Honoré. It's delicious.
PAOLINO: I'm licking my fingers already. I can't wait for the party to begin.
TOTO: I didn't mean that. Don't get angry. I was just telling you so you'd see why I was late. I had to get it all ready for you—Look. (*Puts the box on the end table and opens it.*)
PAOLINO: But . . . (*Gives a high sign.*)
TOTO: Relax. It's a real wonder, because it can't miss. See . . . half is white—vanilla—that part is for the boy . . . and for you, if you want to try it. The brown half, the chocolate cream . . . don't let the kid near that stuff, I'm warning you. Watch out.
PAOLINO: The chocolate, right. But . . . (*Looks at him meaningfully again.*)
TOTO: Don't worry!
PAOLINO: Fine, then you'd better be going. It's getting late. The ship is already in. Go and say a little prayer—and let's hope for the best.
TOTO: You can count on it.
PAOLINO: I'd better be able to count on it. (*Suddenly goes pale.*) For the love of God, I can trust you, can't I?
TOTO: How can you doubt it?
PAOLINO: You're a real friend. And the coffee I give you in the morning—you can count on it from now on. Now get out of here.
TOTO: Of course. And thanks. Good-bye, Paolino. (*He exits by the left door.*)
PAOLINO: (*He picks up the cake to place it—with a priestly solemnity—in the middle of the dining room table, at the altar of the beast, and holds it elevated like a consecrated host.*) Oh, God! Do what has to be done. The fate of an entire family, the life and honor of a woman, my total existence—all are hanging in the balance here.
MRS. PERELLA: (*Returning from her room at right, even more full of shame than before. With her back to Paolino, her head lowered, her eyes to the ground, both hands folded to hide her breasts. The neckline of her blouse is very low and she has made the curls as Paolino directed, one in the middle of her forehead and the others on her cheeks.*) Paolino.
PAOLINO: (*Going to her.*) So, you did it. Good for you! Let me see.
MRS. PERELLA: (*Evading him.*) No, no, I'll die of shame. No.
PAOLINO: If you're like this now, how are you going to act in front of him?

Why have you bothered with all of this, then. Here, take your hands away.
MRS. PERELLA: No . . . no.
PAOLINO: But you don't understand—he has to be able to see you? (*She puts her hands to her face, raising her arms from here to there to cover, as much as possible, her exposed breasts.*)
MRS. PERELLA: There, you see.
PAOLINO: Oh . . . fi . . . fine . . . yes . . . it's fi . . . fine . . . (*Realizing that it isn't fine, Mrs. Perella, with her face still hidden, breaks into tears.*) Are you crying? Now stop. You mustn't—you look very nice. If you keep on crying your eyes will get red. (*Suddenly seeing her point of view and embracing her.*) Darling, please forgive me. You have to know that I'm suffering more than you are for this awful mess. I'd rather kill myself, believe me, than have to witness this spectacle of virtue prostituting itself. This is your martyrdom—and you have to face it courageously. It's my job to give you that courage.
MRS. PERELLA: Then at least help me.
PAOILINO: That's impossible. I have to persuade you to do it. If not, any help I offer is useless. Now smile . . . smile. Try to make yourself smile.
MRS. PERELLA: But how, Paolino!
PAOLINO: How . . . like this . . . look. (*He smiles a cold, grimacing smile.*)
MRS. PERELLA: But I can't, not like that.
PAOLINO: Of course you can. Look. What does it take to make you laugh. A little monkey business? (*He does some antics, including imitating a chimp.*) See, look. Yes, like that, yes, you're laughing. I scratch myself, see. (*She laughs through her tears with a convulsive laugh.*) Laugh—yes—just like that. That's terrific. Keep on laughing. Look, now I'll throw myself on the ground, like a big cat. (*He does it and her laughter increases.*) Wonderful—laugh even louder. Now I'll butt like a billygoat. (*He does it and her convulsive laugh almost becomes a spasm.*) Long live the animal kingdom! Long live the beasts!
MRS. PERELLA: (*As he continues to butt and she hurts from laughing.*) That's enough! Please! I can't take it anymore. (*She suddenly shifts from her laughter to a desperate sigh.*)
PAOLINO: (*Stops his animal act at once and runs to her frantically.*) You're crying again! You were laughing so nicely. I know how you feel. But stop, for God's sake. You'll drive me crazy. (*In the grip of a growing frenzy he pulls her blouse down angrily and then forcefully replaces it, like a doll that falls to pieces in one's hands.*) Now sit down and be quiet. Don't say a word and don't move. I have to paint you up.
MRS. PERELLA: (*Stunned, terrified and mortified by what he's done.*) Paint me up?
PAOLINO: Yes. (*Makes her sit on the chair by the end table, with her back to the audience.*) Dry your eyes now. Look at your cheeks—you're as pale as a ghost. You've no color at all. Do you think that beast will appreciate the delicacy of your subtle beauty or the sweetness of your melancholy grace! I have to

paint you up. Lift your face . . . like this. (*He raises it.*)
MRS. PERELLA: (*Like an automaton, keeping her face raised, while Paolino gets the makeup from the table.*) All right, do whatever you want.
PAOLINO: (*Begins to make her up, laying it on thickly around her cheeks, eyes and mouth with frightening exaggeration.*) Now, wait. First the cheeks, like this. Remember, it's all for his sake. Since this is the only kind of woman he understands, you'll have to look like this. Now the mouth . . . where's the lipstick? Here it is—purse your lips a little—like this—fine. Don't start crying again, for God's sake. Everything will run. Now the eyes . . . I have to make them black. I have everything here I need. Now close your eyes—close them. Now, like this—okay—now to use a little pencil on the eyebrows. Just . . . like . . . this. Let's see how you look now. (*Mrs. Perella is almost staring wildly. She gets up and we see a face exaggeratedly made up, like a street slut.*)
PAOLINO: (*Like he's drunk from an orgasm, with a grotesque air of triumph.*) And now, Mr. Captain Perella, tell me what you see in your lady from Naples?
MRS. PERELLA: (*After remaining in place for a while, like she's on display in a booth at a fair, she goes and looks at herself in the mirror over the couch. She's horrified at what she sees.*) Oh, God—I look awful.
PAOLINO: You're exactly what you have to be for him. (*He begins to clean up and remove all the stuff he used to make her up.*)
MRS. PERELLA: But it's no longer me. He won't even recognize me.
PAOLINO: That's not important. He has to see you like this.
MRS. PERELLA: In this horrible mask?
PAOLINO: It's exactly what he wants to see.
MRS. PERELLA: But what about Nono? What kind of mother does this make me, Paolino.
PAOLINO: (*On the brink of tears, embracing her.*) Of course you're right, my poor darling. But what else can we do. He wants you like this. He doesn't want you as the mother of his child. You have to wear this grotesque mask to appeal to his bestiality. Underneath you're still the same, no matter how much you suffer. You're the same for yourself and for me—and our love for each other can't be touched by it!
NONO'S VOICE: (*From offstage.*) Papa's home! Papa's home!
PAOLINO: (*Disengaging himself from Mrs. Perella at once and moving away from her.*) Here he is. Now act the way I told you to.
MRS. PERELLA: Oh, God . . . Oh, God.
PAOLINO: Smile, my dear, smile.
NONO'S VOICE: (*Still offstage.*) Papa's here. (*He enters with a nice new soccer ball that is a gift from his father. Once he's onstage, he doesn't speak, as he's too intent on playing.*)
CAPTAIN PERELLA: (*Enters after Nono, snorting like an enormous, bristling wild boar. To Nono, who's busy with the ball, which he has kicked in back of his father.*) Nono,

don't bounce that thing in here or I'll smack you.
MRS. PERELLA: (*With a shout, receiving Nono in her arms.*) Oh, Nono.
PAOLINO: Have you done anything wrong, Nono?
CAPTAIN PERELLA: He hasn't done anything. Listen, when I wasn't even six years old, you know what my father did to punish me because I couldn't swim? He picked me up by the back of the neck and threw me into the ocean, with all my clothes on, shouting from the pier, "Either swim or drown."
PAOLINO: And you didn't drown?
CAPTAIN PERELLA: Of course not. I learned how to swim. I'm telling you this because I don't agree with your teaching methods. You're too easy with the kid, too soft.
PAOLINO: Me, soft? I beg your pardon, but I'm not. Of course I believe in the need . . .
CAPTAIN PERELLA: What need! It's a question of character. I say that you're too soft and the proof is the way you've spoiled the kid.
PAOLINO: (*Suddenly heating up.*) Now look here, captain, you're wrong. It's not my place to say so, but the problem lies elsewhere and you should know where I mean.
CAPTAIN PERELLA: You mean his mother?
PAOLINO: No, of course it's not his mother. If Nono is spoiled, it's because he's an only child.
CAPTAIN PERELLA: What only child? You don't know what you're talking about.
PAOLINO: Then he's not an only child?
CAPTAIN PERELLA: (*Strongly, getting riled.*) You have to know how to raise them.
PAOLINO: Well, of course. But if there were two of them . . .
CAPTAIN PERELLA: (*Infuriated, with blood in his eye.*) Don't say that, not even as a joke. One is enough!
PAOLINO: (*Suddenly backing off.*) Calm down, for God's sake. Don't get upset. I was just using it as an excuse.
CAPTAIN PERELLA: Another son. That's all I need. (*While this dialogue has been occurring, there is another silent dialogue in back, between Nono and his mother. Nono, pretending to cry, goes to her and then seeing her made up as she is, suddenly stops, with his eyes wide open. Meanwhile she puts her hands together in prayer that he doesn't scream out his shock and disbelief. Then, assaulted by her customary visceral contraction, her mouth opens wide like a fish and she immediately puts her handkerchief to her mouth, leaving Nono frightened into throwing his hands into the air.*) Come here, Nono. (*He says this in a penitential way. Then he turns and discovers him in the act of tossing up his hands.*) What are you doing? (*Looks toward his wife.*) What's the matter? (*Discovers her made up and dressed the way she is.*) Oh my God. Look at you! (*He erupts into interminable, obstreperous, cynical laughter, during which*

Paolino, in back of him, clenches his fists, convulsed with anger. He opens his hands and restrains himself from the temptation to pounce on Perella and strangle him. Meanwhile Mrs. Perella, humiliated and terrified, looks at the ground.) Look at the way you're plastered over. Ha, ha, ha, ha, ha! Like a monkey . . . Ha, ha, ha, ha. You're made up like an organ grinder's monkey, I swear. *(Takes her hand and contemplates her while he's still laughing. Then he sees her exposed bosom.)* Look at this. What's this all about? *(Turning to Paolino.)* Hey, professor . . . ha, ha, ha, ha . . . Have you had a look at this?

PAOLINO: *(Trying to hold back his indignation.)* Not . . . not at all . . . why should I? It seems to me that the lady has . . . has taken a certain amount of care . . .

CAPTAIN PERELLA: Care! You call this care! This disguise she's got on. *(Pointing to her neckline.)* And dishing out everything she's got, like this. Ha, ha, ha, ha!

MRS. PERELLA: Francesco, please, forgive me.

CAPTAIN PERELLA: You didn't do all this for my sake, did you? No, you couldn't have! Oh, for crying out loud, no. *(Points to her breasts.)* Well, you can close up shop now. I'm not buying anything! *(Turns to Paolino.)* That stuff is all in the past for me. I don't have my taste for it anymore. *(To his wife.)* Thank you dear, thank you. Now go and wash that crap off your face. I'm starving. I want to eat—right away.

MRS. PERELLA: Everything is ready, Francesco.

CAPTAIN PERELLA: Good. Can we sit down? Are you joining us, professor?

PAOLINO: Uh, yes, I think so.

MRS. PERELLA: Yes, Francesco, I invited him to stay . . .

CAPTAIN PERELLA: It's fine with me. Come on, professor, take a seat. Now, don't be shocked, because when I eat, I eat, if you know what I mean. As you well can see. *(Points to his belly, then turns to his wife, who is about to sit across from him.)* No dear, please—listen, if you're not going to wash that stuff off, then don't sit across from me, mucked up like that. I'll just start laughing again and I won't be able to swallow. What made you do this to yourself?

MRS. PERELLA: Francesco, why must there be something behind this?

CAPTAIN PERELLA: Well then, how did you end up like this? *(Makes a gesture to signify if it was some kind of whim—and then he laughs.)* Ha, ha, ha, ha. But tell me, professor, were you serious about what you said?

PAOLINO: Of course I was. Can't you see that your wife is very attractive this way?

CAPTAIN PERELLA: Attractive. Sure. I don't deny it. If she were a . . . you know what I mean. But as my wife, no. In fact, as my wife she's, to tell the honest truth, ridiculous! *(Begins to laugh again.)* I can't control myself. Bear with me, professor. I'm going to have her sit next to you and you can sit facing me.

PAOLINO: *(Getting up and taking her place.)* Whatever you say.

CAPTAIN PERELLA: Sorry to bother you . . . Thanks. (*To his wife.*) Now can we eat? (*Turns to Nono who is pouting and sitting resolutely on the couch.*) Nono, come to the table.
NONO: No.
CAPTAIN PERELLA: (*Bangs his fist on the table.*) Get over here this instant. Don't make me say it again.
PAOLINO: Please, Nono, come and sit down like a good boy.
CAPTAIN PERELLA: (*Banging the other fist.*) Stop that!
PAOLINO: Sorry, sorry.
CAPTAIN PERELLA: You're spoiling him, like I told you. He has to learn how to obey, without being coaxed. I said get over here—right now. And I mean it!
MRS. PERELLA: (*While the captain is doing that, almost in tears, softly to Paolino.*) My God, my God.
PAOLINO: (*Softly replying to her.*) Be brave. Now smile—look at me—like this.
CAPTAIN PERELLA: (*Setting Nono forcefully on a chair at the table.*) There. Now you'll sit there and because you've been a bad boy, you won't eat. From now on, when I say move, you move—or you'll get it. (*Threatens to hit him and Nono, frightened, sits up straight in his chair.*) That's better. Now you stay like that. (*Turns to his wife.*) Are we ever going to eat around here?
MRS. PERELLA: (*Seeing Grazia enter from the kitchen with a steaming soup tureen.*) Here it is, Francesco. Right away. (*Grazia serves from the credenza to the table and will exit and return several times during the meal.*)
CAPTAIN PERELLA: About time! (*To Paolino, who after the lecture to Mrs. Perella has maintained an involuntary smile plastered on his face.*) Listen, professor, I'm saying this to you as a friend. I would really appreciate it if you wouldn't grin like that when I discipline my son or my wife.
PAOLINO: Me? Grin? Me?
CAPTAIN PERELLA: Yes, you. Your mouth is making a grin even now.
PAOLINO: Really. Am I grinning?
CAPTAIN PERELLA: Yes, you're grinning.
PAOLINO: Oh, God. And I didn't even realize it, captain, I swear. I'm afraid that it wasn't really me, because, I assure you, I wasn't grinning.
CAPTAIN PERELLA: But how could you not be grinning, if you're grinning?
PAOLINO: Am I still doing it? You've got to believe me—it's not me. Grinning is the last thing in the world I want to do at this moment. If I'm grinning it must be . . . what can I say . . . it must be involuntary . . . yes . . . my nerves acting on their own account.
CAPTAIN PERELLA: You have nerves that make you act like this?
PAOLINO: It certainly looks that way, doesn't it.
CAPTAIN PERELLA: I've never heard of such a thing.
PAOLINO: Neither have I. Not until now. But as you see, today—it just happened—like this—nerves . . . (*They begin to eat—pause.*)

NONO: *(To whom Grazia has just dished out some soup.)* Can I eat, papa?
CAPTAIN PERELLA: I told you no. *(To his wife.)* Who served him?
MRS. PERELLA: Grazia did, Francesco.
CAPTAIN PERELLA: She shouldn't have.
PAOLINO: But really, she didn't know.
CAPTAIN PERELLA: Then she *(pointing to wife)* should have told her. *(To Nono.)* All right. This time you can eat. *(Nono wriggles on his chair without touching the soup.)*
MRS. PERELLA: Go ahead, Nono, eat. *(Nono makes his customary finger gesture.)*
CAPTAIN PERELLA: What does that mean?
NONO: I wasn't talking about the soup, papa.
CAPTAIN PERELLA: And what were you talking about. Right now we're eating soup.
NONO: *(Hesitatingly, roguishly.)* Well, I see something else.
MRS. PERELLA: *(In a lamentful tone.)* What is it now, Nono?
PAOLINO: Now, be a good boy . . .
NONO: *(Points, with a quiet gesture that is retracted immediately, at the cake in the middle of the table.)* There it is!
CAPTAIN PERELLA: What is it? Oh, it's a cake.
PAOLINO: Exactly . . . I beg your pardon, captain.
CAPTAIN PERELLA: Oh, did you bring it?
PAOLINO: Yes, I did . . . I'm sorry to say . . . if you'll excuse me.
CAPTAIN PERELLA: Excuse you, why? It's beautiful. Why should you apologize for bringing me a cake like that as a gift. I should be the one to thank you, instead, professor.
PAOLINO: No, I should thank you, captain.
CAPTAIN PERELLA: For inviting you to dinner? All right. Then we should all thank each other—one at a time.
PAOLINO: *(With an interjection that escapes spontaneously.)* Oh, let's hope so.
CAPTAIN PERELLA: Hope? . . . What do you mean?
PAOLINO: *(Trying to remedy his mistake.)* Er . . . that . . . you'll enjoy it. I mean, let's hope that . . . that it's good.
NONO: I know I'll like it. *(Kneels on his chair.)* Especially this chocolate part.
CAPTAIN PERELLA: Sit down, Nono! *(Nono obeys.)*
PAOLINO: *(In a cold sweat.)* Now don't make trouble, Nono. We're not going to start with the chocolate part—and if you insist, you'll make me sorry I ever brought it. In fact, you can't even taste the chocolate part.
NONO: Why?
PAOLINO: Because your mama told me that . . . that you haven't been feeling well lately . . . isn't that right, Mrs. Perella . . . that it's been your stomach . . . and right now chocolate would be . . .
NONO: But I feel fine. I don't have a stomachache, mama.
PAOLINO: *(Sharply.)* Nono.

MRS. PERELLA: (*In another tone.*) Nono.
CAPTAIN PERELLA: (*In still another tone.*) Nono! Now stop it!
PAOLINO: I had it made up this way on purpose, my boy, half and half . . .
NONO: But I love chocolate.
CAPTAIN PERELLA: And you can have it. So just be quiet. Anyway, I don't care for chocolate.
PAOLINO: (*In a sudden panic.*) What! You don't like chocolate?!
CAPTAIN PERELLA: No, not really . . . not very much. I prefer the vanilla . . .
PAOLINO: (*Feeling his spirit collapsing.*) Oh, God . . .
CAPTAIN PERELLA: What's the matter?
PAOLINO: Nothing . . . nothing. I see that . . . I was . . . that I made a mistake.
CAPTAIN PERELLA: Don't worry about it. I eat anything. But right now the only thing we seem to be eating is words. Where's Grazia? What the hell is she doing? (*Pounds the table.*) What's going on around here? (*Grazia returns with the next course.*)
MRS. PERELLA: Here she is now, Francesco.
CAPTAIN PERELLA: (*To Grazia.*) I want to be served right away. I've told you a thousand times that I hate to wait when I'm eating. Give me that. (*Grabs the serving platter from her hands with such violence that the contents are splattered all over the place. He springs to his feet, throwing the platter on the table and breaking it, along with several plates and glasses.*) For God's sake, now look what you've done.
GRAZIA: If you hadn't snatched it from me . . .
CAPTAIN PERELLA: But you dumped it all over the table, you animal. The rest of you can eat—I've lost my appetite. (*He's about to leave for his room.*)
PAOLINO: (*Runs after him.*) No, look, please, captain . . .
MRS. PERELLA: (*Also pursuing him.*) For heaven's sake, Francesco, remember that we have a dinner guest.
CAPTAIN PERELLA: (*To Paolino.*) As you can see, professor, I'm cursed. I'm cursed in my own home.
PAOLINO: Calm down, I beg you.
CAPTAIN PERELLA: Why should I calm down. It's like they do it on purpose.
MRS. PERELLA: We try to do everything to make you happy.
CAPTAIN PERELLA: (*Noticing her face, made up as it is, once again.*) Look at that face, look at it.
PAOLINO: Come, now, her face seems fine to me, captain. I am a friend of the family, it's true, but after all, you did invite me to stay for dinner . . .
CAPTAIN PERELLA: All right then, for your sake. But I can't guarantee we'll make it through to the end of the meal.
PAOLINO: Don't even think about such things. Let's just hope . . . let's hope there won't be anything else to upset us . . .
CAPTAIN PERELLA: Do you know what you're asking for? I can't remember

the last time I was able to finish a meal here, in my own home. (*Turning to his wife.*) It's useless, you know, to keep reminding me that we have a dinner guest. When I get mad, professor, you've got to excuse me, but I lose sight of everything and it doesn't matter who's here or isn't here. To avoid a scene I have to leave. (*While this has been going on, Nono, remaining at the table, has knelt on his chair, and like a cat with his paw, has tasted the cake, i.e., the chocolate part.*) Look there, see, exactly what I've been talking about. Is that the way to raise a kid? (*He picks Nono up by the ear and pulls him to the door at right.*) Go to bed this minute. No supper for you tonight. Just go to bed. (*As soon as they reach the door Perella pushes him in with his foot.*) Get out of here! (*Returns to the table.*) See, it never fails. This is what happens every time I try to have a meal in this house.

MRS. PERELLA: He's a good boy. (*To Paolino.*) What difference does it make that he's had a little taste.

PAOLINO: But it could make a big difference. A little here, a little there.

CAPTAIN PERELLA: You'd better not even let me look at that damned cake, professor. I'll be tempted to take it and throw it out there. (*Indicates the veranda.*)

PAOLINO: (*Protecting it.*) No, for God's sake. That would be a grave insult—to me.

CAPTAIN PERELLA: All right. Then let's eat it. Right away.

PAOLINO: Right away. What an excellent idea. If you'll allow me, I'll cut it and then serve it. Right away. Here we are. Right away. (*Cuts and serves it.*) For the lady, first—here you are.

MRS. PERELLA: Oh, that's much too much.

PAOLINO: What do you mean, too much? (*Turns to the captain.*) Now, if you'll allow me—notice I say, if you'll allow me, because if not then I won't. As a teacher I must always look out for such things . . .

CAPTAIN PERELLA: What about Nono?

PAOLINO: No, none for him today. You punished him and you were right. I'll tell you what. Let's cut a slice for him and if it's all right with you he can have it tomorrow. This whole vanilla section. I promised it to him as a reward, as his teacher.

CAPTAIN PERELLA: (*Hitting the table with his fist, happy and self-absorbed with the nonsense he's about to utter.*) See, see! Didn't I tell you that your way was too soft . . . much too soft!

PAOLINO: (*Laughing coldly, while Mrs. Perella does the same.*) Oh, yes . . . of course. Now, with this half, we'll do like this . . .

CAPTAIN PERELLA: What are you doing? All that for me? Don't.

PAOLINO: I insist. You see—the cream—it . . . you know . . . how can I say it . . . it makes me . . . it gives me indigestion . . . so the less of it I eat the better . . . and you've had so little to eat so far . . .

CAPTAIN PERELLA: (*Eating a big mouthful.*) It's good—very good. Excellent

choice, professor.
PAOLINO: You can't know how happy you're making me at this moment.
MRS. PERELLA: Me too, when I see you eat like this, with so much gusto.
PAOLINO: Have another piece? Look, I haven't touched it yet.
CAPTAIN PERELLA: No . . . please.
PAOLINO: Come on. It will just upset my stomach.
CAPTAIN PERELLA: If I have any more, it will be a little bit of Nono's piece. That looks like too much for him.
PAOLINO: No, really, I can't tell you how happy it would make me if you would take my piece.
CAPTAIN PERELLA: Oh, well—if it makes you sick. Give it here. (*Takes it and eats it as well.*) No way it's gonna bother me. I could eat twice, no three times that much and it wouldn't affect me one bit. (*To his wife.*) Now, what do we have to drink?
MRS. PERELLA: Why . . . I don't know . . .
CAPTAIN PERELLA: Isn't there even a little Marsala.
MRS. PERELLA: We don't have a thing, Francesco.
CAPTAIN PERELLA: (*In a fury, turning to Paolino in order to abandon his wife as usual and shut himself in his room.*) See what kind of wife I have. She invites a guest to dinner and doesn't even make sure that we have a little Marsala in the house.
PAOLINO: Listen, if it's for me . . .
CAPTAIN PERELLA: It's the principle of the thing. This house lacks every thing—foresight, order, good management. All the lady can think about is dolling herself up.
MRS. PERELLA: (*Hurt.*) Me?
CAPTAIN PERELLA: No? Can you deny it?
MRS. PERELLA: But it's the first time, Francesco.
CAPTAIN PERELLA: (*Pulls the table cloth, taking with it everything that's on top and springing to his feet as he does so*) Goddammit!
PAOLINO: (*Fearful.*) Captain, captain.
CAPTAIN PERELLA: She dares to talk back to me like that.
MRS. PERELLA: What did I say?
CAPTAIN PERELLA: Big deal, so it's the first time. Well, it will also be the last. Because as far as I'm concerned, it's a waste of time. Don't even come near me. I'd rather throw myself out the window. Go to hell! (*As he is saying this he runs into his room, enters, slams the door and bolts it—the sound of the bolt being grotesquely exaggerated.*)

(*Both Paolino and Mrs. Perella remain, almost in a trance, while all of this is happening.*)

GRAZIA: (*Enters from the kitchen, sees the mess, throws her hands in the air and shakes*

her head.) Like always, huh?
MRS. PERELLA: (*Responds as soon as she sees the shaking of her head.*) That will be all for now, Grazia. You can clean it up in the morning. (*Nods toward her husband's room.*) He's not making a sound.
GRAZIA: Should I light the fire?
MRS. PERELLA: No, just go.
GRAZIA: (*Making her exit.*) It's like this every time he's home. (*Leaves through the kitchen.*)

(*The moonlight is now starting to come, little by little, through the window opening on the veranda—mainly lighting the five flowerpots on the stand between the two left hand doors.*)

MRS. PERELLA: Did you hear him? He said he'd rather throw himself out the window.
PAOLINO: We just have to wait and see.
MRS. PERELLA: Are you still hopeful? I don't think we have any chance at all, Paolino.
PAOLINO: Both brothers, the doctor and the druggist, told me not to worry, that it was a sure thing.
MRS. PERELLA: But what about him? You don't really know him, Paolino. He *really* would rather throw himself out the window.
PAOLINO: Listen, if you'd rather, we can take the beast to court.
MRS. PERELLA: I'll wait here—all night if I have to.
PAOLINO: But you have to wait with faith.
MRS. PERELLA: But it's useless. I know it is.
PAOLINO: You must have at least a little faith. If you do, you can help attract him. I really do believe in what they say about spiritual power. And you must too. We don't have any choice. If this doesn't work, the abyss is yawning open right in front of us. I have no idea what we could do next. Not even where to start.
MRS. PERELLA: Look, I'll sit here, like this. (*She sits in an old armchair, facing the door of her husband's room, so that he'll find her in front of it—in the pose of "Ecce Ancilla Domini" bathed in the moonlight.*)
PAOLINO: That's perfect. You're a saint, you truly are. Now we have to work out a signal for tomorrow. I know. I'll come to the front of the house first thing in the morning—at dawn. I certainly won't get a minute's sleep tonight, that's for sure. If the answer is yes, you have to give me some kind of signal. Here, look, put one of these flowerpots here in the veranda window, so I can see it from the street. Do you understand? (*He stands a moment in the position of the angel making the Annunciation, with a flowerpot in his hand. The pot contains a gigantic lily. The moonlight gives it a cold luminosity.*)
MRS. PERELLA: I'll wait here. Until tomorrow, Paolino.
PAOLINO: As you wish. (*He leaves.*)

END OF ACT II

ACT III

The same setting as Act II. It is dawn of the following day. There is no flowerpot on the veranda windowsill. The tablecloth and the remains of the mess made by Captain Perella are still on the floor. As the curtain rises Grazia is discovered totally absorbed in cleaning up, bent over picking up the debris on the floor and placing it, little by little, on the table. From time to time she straightens up, stretches out and contracts her face to show that her back is killing her. She then makes a fist and shakes it in the direction of the captain's room and mutters an unintelligible imprecation.

GRAZIA: Just look at this mess! Broken plates and glasses everywhere. That poor tablecloth. A pigsty would be too good for that man. Well, I see at least one bottle survived the fray. I can't take much more of this. (*The doorbell rings.*) Who could that be at this hour? (*Goes to answer the door, she gestures toward the captain's room, mutters something and exits into the kitchen. She returns shortly with the sailor.*) But I tell you Mrs. Perella hasn't left anything for you.

SAILOR: Then the captain isn't sailing today?

GRAZIA: How am I supposed to know if he's sailing or not?

SAILOR: But he's got to sail today. And Mrs. Perella should have gotten his gear ready last night.

GRAZIA: Last night! She really was in the mood to think of his gear last night.

SAILOR: They had a big fight?

GRAZIA: And how.

SAILOR: Oh. And he broke everything, as usual.
GRAZIA: What do you mean as usual. Like I've never heard or seen before.
SAILOR: Really? What did he do?
GRAZIA: What did he do? He . . .
SAILOR: Go on, tell me.
GRAZIA: (*Giving him a sign.*) I don't know.
SAILOR: Must have mistreated the missus, I figure. And been nasty to the kid. Did he take it out on you too?
GRAZIA: (*Looks at him and is about to say something and then stops short.*) Let me get on with my work.
SAILOR: You too, huh. Ooh. Some get sugar and some get shit. Some dish it out and others have to take it on the chin.
GRAZIA: What are you talking about?
SAILOR: You know. (*Mimes beating someone up.*) Here he gives it good. But from the other one—in Naples . . . Here he may be the wolf, but with that one he's as gentle as a lamb.
GRAZIA: A lamb? (*Softly.*) A pig, that's what he is.
SAILOR: You're right. But the other one knows how to handle him. I know. I've been with him ever since I went to sea. I've been to the other place several times. Every time he's in Naples. Have I seen things there! It's the exact opposite of here. That one really lets him have it. You should see her—she's something else. She weighs at least 200 pounds. And ugly. Who knows what he sees in her. What a disaster. And a baby a year. She's already had five—no, make that six, by now.
GRAZIA: Is she young?
SAILOR: Yeah, she's still young. Not even thirty yet.
GRAZIA: And it's not enough?
SAILOR: For whom? For her!
GRAZIA: For him. I mean him.
SAILOR: You mean because he has a wife here as well?
GRAZIA: What wife. He doesn't even look at this one.
SAILOR: Really. There isn't anyone else you know of, is there.
GRAZIA: (*Laughing.*) Ha, ha, ha, ha . . . That would really be funny. Why don't you get out of here.
SAILOR: I'm leaving, don't worry. But I'll be back later. And tell the missus I came for his gear—and that she better get it ready. See you later, eh?
GRAZIA: Fine. Later. (*He leaves through the kitchen. She returns and tries to find if any unbroken plates or glasses might be hidden in the folds of the tablecloth. She finds some and puts them on the table, repeating her backache gesture. A few seconds later we hear—again grotesquely exaggerated—the sound of the bolt of the captain's room.*) So here he is. The wild beast coming out of his cage.
CAPTAIN PERELLA: (*Enters, still sleepy, with slits for eyes, in an even fiercer mood than ever. He sees Grazia on the floor.*) So it's you. Who were you talking with?

GRAZIA: The sailor.
CAPTAIN PERELLA: He gone?
GRAZIA: He just left.
CAPTAIN PERELLA: Why was he here so early?
GRAZIA: He came to get your gear for the ship. (*Pause.*)
CAPTAIN PERELLA: Don't you even wish your master a good morning?
GRAZIA: Sure. I really have the time for that. This here—this is my "good morning." (*Points to the mess on the floor.*)
CAPTAIN PERELLA: You still cleaning up? What did you do all last night? (*She gives him a long, cold stare and returns to her cleaning without responding.*) Answer me. (*He looms over her menacingly.*)
GRAZIA: (*Gets up, looks at him, then speaks.*) You're asking *me* what did I do? (*Brief pause.*) You smashed, you broke, you (*underlining in an ambiguous way*) made the help, whose duties do not include . . .
CAPTAIN PERELLA: Bring me some coffee, right now.
GRAZIA: I haven't made any yet.
CAPTAIN PERELLA: (*Raising himself up, with his hands in the air.*) Is that how you speak to me?
GRAZIA: Don't you take another step closer. If you lay a hand on me, I'll scream my head off.
CAPTAIN PERELLA: Just go make the coffee—NOW! You know I want it ready as soon as I get out of bed.
GRAZIA: And how was I supposed to know that you'd be up at the crack of dawn this morning. After what . . .
CAPTAIN PERELLA: Are you finished? Now go and get my coffee, right away!
GRAZIA: I'm going, don't worry. (*She exits left.*)
CAPTAIN PERELLA: (*Holds his head.*) Let me think for a minute. (*With his face more ominous and disgusted than ever, the eyes hollow and cruel, he thinks. Then he snorts, frenetically rumples his clothes and accompanies the act with a kind of bestial roar in his throat. He shakes his head and walks around the room, chomping at the bit. He's on fire. He can't breathe. He goes back to the veranda and stares through the rear window. Once he sees the ocean he gets his breath back. Then he glances down to the street below and discovers Paolino. He makes a gesture of surprise and leans out to speak to him.*) Hey, professor. What are you doing out there—at this hour? (*Leans out to hear him.*) What? I see—a little air. Yes, this breeze is delightful. Do you want to come up? Come on—you can have a cup of coffee with me. It's no trouble. Please, come on up. (*He remains on the veranda for a few moments and then goes to greet Paolino, who enters from the kitchen with an expression of mortal anguish, black circles under his eyes, gleaming with madness, as if, not having seen the signal on the veranda, he's contemplating a serious crime.*) How did you get here so fast. Did you jump up from the street?
PAOLINO: Yes. Tell me. Did you see me coming from the docks?
CAPTAIN PERELLA: I happened to look down and saw you looking up at me.

PAOLINO: I was on my way back from the docks. When I passed your house the first time there was a crowd of people and they were shouting about something. Tell me—by any chance could something have fallen from that window . . . on the veranda . . . like a flowerpot?

CAPTAIN PERELLA: (*Taken aback.*) A flowerpot. Onto the street?

PAOLINO: Yes, from that window.

CAPTAIN PERELLA: Not that I know of.

PAOLINO: No?

CAPTAIN PERELLA: I don't know what you're talking about. Why do you ask?

PAOLINO: Because it seemed that . . . down there, under the window, in the midst of that crowd . . . there was a pile of . . . I don't know, shards . . . and I figured that's why they were shouting.

CAPTAIN PERELLA: I didn't hear anything.

PAOLINO: And there wasn't a flowerpot there when you went over to the window.

CAPTAIN PERELLA: Nothing. Look, there are the flowerpots. All five of them.

PAOLINO: Only five.

CAPTAIN PERELLA: Yes, just five. Can't you see. There's only room for five.

PAOLINO: (*Almost to himself, grieving, freezing up.*) Oh, then forget it . . . (*Interrupting himself again to look even more intently into Perella's face.*)

CAPTAIN PERELLA: (*Eyeing him.*) What's the matter—you almost seem disappointed that none of the flowerpots fell over.

PAOLINO: It's nothing—it's just that I figured . . . that it had to be one of your flowerpots.

CAPTAIN PERELLA: Because you heard the crowd in the street shouting?

PAOLINO: You know how it is when you imagine something. I thought it was real, as if I passed some people and heard them yelling—"there was a flowerpot—they told me—in the captain's window up there, and it must have fallen."

CAPTAIN PERELLA: But there wasn't any flowerpot. And come to think of it, it's strange that I didn't hear any shouting from down there.

PAOLINO: Let's forget about it. Excuse me, but you . . . (*He interrupts himself as if he has just noticed some significant sign in the captain's facial expression.*)

CAPTAIN PERELLA: (*Disturbed, but not comprehending.*) Me . . . what?

PAOLINO: Yes, I said . . . you . . . (*He pauses again to study the captain's face more intently.*)

CAPTAIN PERELLA: What is it?—You know that you're looking at me in a very strange way?

PAOLINO: No, it's nothing, nothing at all. It's just that I see . . . yes, I see . . .

CAPTAIN PERELLA: What do you see?

PAOLINO: Nothing, no—I see that—that you got up early, that's all.

CAPTAIN PERELLA: Yes. But you must have gotten up even earlier, if you're already out of the house and over here, on your way home from the docks.

PAOLINO: Yes . . . I . . . I . . . I got up early too.
CAPTAIN PERELLA: (*Looks at him and breaks into laughter.*) You're looking pretty strange this morning.
PAOLINO: I'm just a little nervous, that's all.
CAPTAIN PERELLA: But you just took a nice long walk. That should make you feel better. It's very healthy to take a walk like that first thing in the morning.
PAOLINO: Very healthy, sure thing. (*To himself.*) I'll kill him. I swear to God, I'll murder him.
CAPTAIN PERELLA: There's nothing better, when you're nervous or upset, than to be outside, in the fresh air. Where all your worries can evaporate.
PAOLINO: Of course. You're absolutely right. I . . . I didn't sleep very well last night and . . .
CAPTAIN PERELLA: Don't talk to me about sleep.
PAOLINO: (*Happy yet nervous.*) You too. You didn't sleep well either?
CAPTAIN PERELLA: (*Angrily.*) I didn't sleep at all!
PAOLINO: (*With rising anxiety.*) Ah . . . and?
CAPTAIN PERELLA: What?
PAOLINO: Well, now that you mention it, I can see you look a little worse for wear.
CAPTAIN PERELLA: I tell you I didn't sleep a wink. What a hellish night. Maybe it was the heat.
PAOLINO: That's it—must have been the heat. It certainly was hot—very hot—sweltering—last night.
CAPTAIN PERELLA: Almost enough to drive you nuts.
PAOLINO: So you must have gotten out of bed, right?
CAPTAIN PERELLA: (*Looks at him.*) Yes, as a matter of fact I did.
PAOLINO: I can imagine. When . . . when the bed begins to feel like it's on fire . . . from the heat . . . your room . . . there . . . it must have seemed like an oven, I suppose.
CAPTAIN PERELLA: That's it exactly—an oven.
PAOLINO: So you had to get out, right?
CAPTAIN PERELLA: (*Torpid, after looking at him.*) Yes, in fact . . . I went out for a while . . . because at one point I thought I was going to suffocate . . . (*He sees Grazia enter with a tray and a cup of coffee.*) Ah, wonderful, here's my coffee. Good girl. But you only brought one cup. What about our guest here?
GRAZIA: (*Frowning, in as uncivil a tone as possible.*) And how am I supposed to know to bring him a cup if no one tells me.
CAPTAIN PERELLA: Don't talk back to me like that. Do you have to be told everything. You certainly take a lot of liberties around here in other matters.
GRAZIA: (*Glares at them and grumbles.*) Liberties! I'm the one taking liberties at this moment, I suppose?

CAPTAIN PERELLA: The impudence of this woman, really. Watch out or I'll toss you out of here on your rear end.
GRAZIA: Throw me out! Who's going to throw me out! You better just hope I don't start shouting and tell everyone about what you've done . . .
PAOLINO: (*Almost to himself, dying from the horrible suspicions that he's entertaining, now looking at the captain, then Grazia.*) Oh, God . . . is it possible?
CAPTAIN PERELLA: Professor, have you been listening to this nonsense?
PAOLINO: I've heard . . . I've seen . . . but . . .
CAPTAIN PERELLA: (*Wanting to put an end to all of this.*) Go and get another cup of coffee. NOW! (*To Paolino.*) Here, take this one, professor.
PAOLINO: No thank you. (*To Grazia.*) Don't bother.
CAPTAIN PERELLA: What do you mean, don't bother. Here, take it.
PAOLINO: No, really. I don't want any. Coffee would just make me sick.
CAPTAIN PERELLA: What are you talking about? (*To Grazia.*) Go and make another cup.
PAOLINO: Please, captain, I'm terribly nervous this morning. Upset . . . agitated . . . nervous.
GRAZIA: Well, what's it to be—yes . . . or no.
CAPTAIN PERELLA: Go to hell! (*Grazia leaves in a rage and then can be heard shouting from the kitchen.*) And stop that noise, do you hear. Or I'll stop it for you.
PAOLINO: Excuse me, captain . . . if you allow a servant too many liberties.
CAPTAIN PERELLA: You can't keep servants around too long, that's the problem. Shouldn't become dependent on them—shouldn't even bother with them at all.
PAOLINO: But it's nice having them around. When they know their place . . . and don't act like they're the masters.
CAPTAIN PERELLA: (*Stupefied at the superior attitude Paolino's taking.*) What are you getting at, professor?
PAOLINO: (*Having trouble controlling himself.*) That I'm amazed . . . Yes, I'm truly . . . I don't know how to say it . . . stupefied.
CAPTAIN PERELLA: At the arrogance of this woman.
PAOLINO: Exactly. And that you . . .
CAPTAIN PERELLA: That I what?
PAOLINO: That you tolerate it. It's incredible that she can talk like that to you. Unbelievable—that she can go so far.
CAPTAIN PERELLA: (*Looks at him sheepishly, then lowers his eyes.*) You're right. It's monstrous. (*Almost humble.*) But I told you why. She's been in the house too long. It's my wife's fault.
PAOLINO: (*About to pounce on this, then restraining himself.*) Oh, really? Your wife is to blame for this as well?
CAPTAIN PERELLA: Absolutely. Because she insists I keep that woman here. Because she was here when Nono was born—and knows where everything in the house is. But the devil can take all of that.

PAOLINO: (*Frigidly.*) Pardon me, but for all of this your wife . . .
CAPTAIN PERELLA: What do you mean, for all of this. You've seen what I have to put up with.
PAOLINO: It still seems wrong to blame her.
CAPTAIN PERELLA: Who else is there to blame? This damned place drives me nuts. It's suffocating me. I feel cursed the minute I set foot in here. I can't even get a night's sleep in peace. And now the heat's against me too. It drives me crazy. And you know what happens when I can't even get some sleep. I become furious.
PAOLINO: I understand. But why blame others for this!
CAPTAIN PERELLA: For what?
PAOLINO: You said you become furious. Why? Who's to blame if it's hot?
CAPTAIN PERELLA: I blame myself. I blame the heat. And I blame everyone else as well. Because I need air . . . I'm used to the open air! (*Calming down.*) It's being on shore, professor. Especially in the summertime. I can't stand being on land—or in houses—the walls, the ceiling—and women . . .
PAOLINO: Even women.
CAPTAIN PERELLA: Especially women. I've had it with them. You know how it is. You travel . . . you're away for such a long time . . . Now I'm not saying that I'm an old man . . . but when I was young . . . women . . . I always had a nice one around. When I wanted one, I had one. But when I didn't . . . (*Laughs proudly.*) I was always in control!
PAOLINO: Always? (*To himself.*) I'll kill him. I'll kill him.
CAPTAIN PERELLA: I always got my own way, if you know what I mean. What about you? Or did you give in without a fight?
PAOLINO: Please, don't drag me into this.
CAPTAIN PERELLA: (*Laughs loudly.*) A little smile, a little gesture.
PAOLINO: (*Friendly.*) Captain, please.
CAPTAIN PERELLA: Ha, ha, ha. I can just see how it was with you. A little humility to make you feel guilty, right. Come on, tell the truth.
PAOLINO: That's enough, captain, please. I had a very bad night.
CAPTAIN PERELLA: (*Still laughing.*) You were the type who was always full of scruples and idealism and convinced you must be in love.
PAOLINO: (*Jumping into action.*) Okay. You want me to tell the truth. Then I'll tell you. If I had a wife . . .
CAPTAIN PERELLA: (*Breaks into an even harsher laughter.*) Ha, ha, ha, ha.
PAOLINO: (*Losing all control.*) Stop laughing, for God's sake. Stop it!
CAPTAIN PERELLA: Why get so angry? Ha, ha, ha, ha. How did we get onto wives? We were talking about women.
PAOLINO: And aren't wives women? What are they then?
CAPTAIN PERELLA: Sure they're women . . . sometimes . . . sure.
PAOLINO: So, at least some of the time. You admit that there are times when a husband should treat his wife like a woman.

CAPTAIN PERELLA: Of course. But she won't make him think about her in that way if he forgets, not like other women.
PAOLINO: A wise husband, however, should never forget.
CAPTAIN PERELLA: You're right. It will occur to him. You, dear professor, you've never had a wife, and for your sake, I hope you never will.
PAOLINO: (*Extremely irritated, looking for a pretext to argue.*) But that contradicts what you just said about me.
CAPTAIN PERELLA: What?
PAOLINO: That I was full of scruples . . . I'm not even sure what kind.
CAPTAIN PERELLA: (*Amazed.*) So, now you want to get married?
PAOLINO: I'm not saying that. I'm just saying that you are deceiving yourself on my account.
CAPTAIN PERELLA: I'm deceiving myself?
PAOLINO: Certainly. And committing the cruelest of injustices at the same time.
CAPTAIN PERELLA: Toward whom? Toward you? Toward wives?
PAOLINO: Exactly—toward wives.
CAPTAIN PERELLA: You're on their side?
PAOLINO: I certainly am.
CAPTAIN PERELLA: Ha, ha, ha, ha. Do you know why? Because you don't have one . . . And I bet you also help yourself to other men's wives. That's why you're on their side.
PAOLINO: You dare to say that to me. You.
CAPTAIN PERELLA: (*Dismayed.*) Hey, professor! (*He'll look more and more dismayed during Paolino's subsequent tirade.*)
PAOLINO: You've insulted me. I'm an honest man. A man with a conscience. A man who lives by the rules and who still finds himself—against his will—in a desperate situation. It's not true that I want to take advantage of other men's wives. Because if it were true, why would I say that a husband shouldn't neglect his wife. By the way, as far as I'm concerned, the husband who does neglect his wife is guilty of a crime. Not just one crime, but several. Not only does he force his poor wife—who in spite of everything can remain a saintly woman—to think less of herself and her integrity—but he also may force a man, another man, to be unhappy for the rest of his life. And this man, who is forced to suffer the martyrdom of all this pain, may end up by losing his freedom, even the possibility of freedom, itself. This is what I have to say to you, Captain Perella!

(*Paolino says all of this with an impetuosity that increases in intensity until he is almost looming over the captain, who listens in astonishment. After a certain point it seems that Paolino will, at any moment, take a gun from his pocket and murder the captain. Then Mrs. Perella appears from the right, terrified, in disarray, with the makeup smeared all over her face. She doesn't have the strength to move or speak.*)

MRS. PERELLA: My God—what's going on here?
CAPTAIN PERELLA: Damned if I know. The professor has been on his high horse discussing husbands and wives.
PAOLINO: Just because I was saying . . .
MRS. PERELLA: Not another word, professor. Instead—look— (*Goes to the flower stand and takes a pot.*) Please help me, I beg you.
PAOLINO: (*Beaming.*) Yes . . . really . . .(*Takes a pot.*) Do you want me to put this on the veranda?
MRS. PERELLA: Yes . . . but give it to me. I'll do it. You take another one—unless you're not feeling well.
PAOLINO: (*With an ugly facial gesture.*) Another one? Not feeling well—what do you mean. I've ne . . . never felt better.
MRS. PERELLA: Then, please. (*She goes to put the pot on the windowsill.*)
PAOLINO: Here we are. Shall I put it here? (*Places it next to the first one.*) Like this?
MRS. PERELLA: Yes, thank you . . . (*She proceeds to take and carry to the window the third and fourth pots, while Paolino, full of disdain and sarcasm, precipitously embraces the captain, who is dumbfounded by all of this.*)
PAOLINO: Oh, please excuse me, captain, excuse me.
CAPTAIN PERELLA: For what?
PAOLINO: For all that nonsense that just spewed forth from my mouth. It was like a spell that came over me. But it's passed now. I'm happy now—very happy—and thank you, captain. I thank you with all my heart. Look how blue the sky is today. What a beautiful day it is—and those (*with stupor that is almost terror*) uh, five, five flowerpots there.
MRS. PERELLA: (*Who has the fifth flowerpot in her hand, containing a lily, showing it bashfully, with her eyes lowered.*) They give back life.
PAOLINO: (*At once.*) To a home. Precisely. Thank you captain. Excuse me, I've truly been a beast.
CAPTAIN PERELLA: (*Scratching his head sententiously.*) Well, professor, we must act like men! (*He touches his chest with his finger several times.*)
PAOLINO: But that's easy for you to say, captain—with a wife like yours—who's virtue incarnate.

END

Olga Ragusa, Da Ponte Professor of Italian at Columbia University, is the author of *Narrative and Drama: Essays in Modern Italian Literature from Verga to Pasolini* and *Luigi Pirandello: An Approach to His Theater*, among others. She has lectured widely in the U.S. and abroad.

Norman A. Bailey has combined teaching, investment banking, and now government service in the National Security Council, with an interest in the theatre, throughout his life. He is the author of many plays that have been produced in university and off-Broadway productions, the best known of which is the one-act musical *Harlequinade*.

Roger W. Oliver is the director of the humanities program for the Next Wave Festival at the Brooklyn Academy of Music. He received his Ph.D. in Drama from Stanford University and has taught dramatic literature and theatre history at New York University since 1974. He is the author of *Dreams of Passion: The Theater of Luigi Pirandello*.

PAJ PLAYSCRIPT SERIES

General Editors: Bonnie Marranca and Gautam Dasgupta

OTHER TITLES IN THE SERIES:

THEATRE OF THE RIDICULOUS/Kenneth Bernard, Charles Ludlam, Ronald Tavel

ANIMATIONS: A TRILOGY FOR MABOU MINES/Lee Breuer

THE RED ROBINS/Kenneth Koch

THE WOMEN'S PROJECT/Penelope Gilliatt, Lavonne Mueller, Rose Leiman Goldemberg, Joyce Aaron-Luna Tarlo, Kathleen Collins, Joan Schenkar, Phyllis Purscell

WORDPLAYS: NEW AMERICAN DRAMA/Maria Irene Fornes, Ronald Tavel, Jean-Claude van Itallie, Richard Nelson, William Hauptman, John Wellman

BEELZEBUB SONATA/Stanislaw I. Witkiewicz

DIVISION STREET AND OTHER PLAYS/Steve Tesich

TABLE SETTINGS/James Lapine

THE PRESIDENT AND EVE OF RETIREMENT/Thomas Bernhard

TWELVE DREAMS/James Lapine

COMEDY OF VANITY AND LIFE-TERMS/Elias Canetti

WORDPLAYS 2: NEW AMERICAN DRAMA/Rochelle Owens, Wallace Shawn, Len Jenkin, Harry Kondoleon, John O'Keefe

THE ENTHUSIASTS/Robert Musil